RIDE OR DIE

BRENDA BARRETT

RIDE OR DIE

A Jamaica Treasures Book/November2024
Published by Jamaica Treasures
Manchester, Jamaica

This is a work of fiction. Names, characters, places, and incidents are either the product of the author's imagination or are used fictitiously. Any resemblance to an actual person or persons, living or dead, events, or locales is entirely coincidental.

ISBN 978-976-97430-2-1

Kenny cleared her throat. "Our kids?"

"Well, yes," Camden said. "We want to have at least two, don't we?"

Kenny nodded. "Yes, when we are married. And speaking of marriage, the two years for reassessment are up. Shouldn't we be discussing that?"

Camden sighed and leaned back in his chair. He had realized that the two years were up; he just didn't want to rush into something that was too important to get wrong. The timing had always been tricky for them—both were busy with their careers, social obligations, and personal goals. But he knew Kenny wasn't just another part of his life; she was the most significant part.

"Yeah, I've been thinking about it a lot," Camden admitted, his eyes meeting hers. "But I want to make sure we're both ready. I don't want to make promises I can't keep or rush into something because of a deadline we set two years ago."

Kenny glared at him. "Two years is not rushing. I need to know that we're moving forward, Camden. That we're not just standing still, waiting for the perfect time that might never come."

ALSO BY BRENDA BARRETT

FULL CIRCLE
NEW BEGINNINGS
THE PREACHER AND THE PROSTITUTE
AFTER THE END
THE EMPTY HAMMOCK
THE PULL OF FREEDOM
REBOUND SERIES
THREE RIVERS SERIES
NEW SONG SERIES
BANCROFT SERIES
MAGNOLIA SISTERS SERIES
SCARLETT SERIES
WILEY BROTHERS SERIES
PRYCE SISTERS SERIES
THE JACKSONS SERIES
CRIMSON HILL SERIES
SPICE AND STONE SERIES
RIDGEVIEW SERIES

ABOUT THE AUTHOR

Brenda Barrett is an award-winning and bestselling author who has a passion for writing real Jamaican romances.

When she's not weaving words that transport readers to exotic locales, you can find her nurturing her green thumb in the garden or doting on her beloved cats.

With an infectious zest for life, this author brings a unique perspective to her writing that is both relatable and thought-provoking.

Don't be surprised if you find yourself lost in the pages of her latest work, as she seamlessly blends romance with some drama, mystery, and suspense, or even sci-fi, leaving readers wanting more.

You can connect with Brenda online at:
Brenalbar.com
Twitter.com/AuthorWriterBB
Facebook.com/AuthorBrendaBarrett

Chapter One

Two Years Ago

It was a double celebration: Camden Byfield's twenty-seventh birthday and housewarming party. The night was perfect; it had rained earlier, and the place was significantly cooler now. A gentle wind was blowing, and she could smell the white roses planted in giant pots on the opposite sides of the patio.

Kenny had excused herself from the joyous occasion inside to take a breather. It wasn't that it was a bad party or even dull. It was her—she felt off, maybe a little sad. What was wrong with her? She should be happy for Camden's successes; this house purchase was a huge deal for him. One more step toward 'adulting,' as he had called it. And she was the one who had set things in motion.

She had casually suggested that Camden buy into the Ridgeview townhouse complex after hearing about it from Richard Tinsdale, the property developer and her client.

When Richard decided to dip his toes into the luxury market, he summoned her and Jewel, his app developers, to his office. "I want some changes to the app," he had told them. "I am going luxury."

It was Richard's first high-end development of six townhouses on a bluff overlooking the sea. He had toyed with several names but eventually settled on Ridgeview.

For the past year, she and Camden had a long-standing date at Freddy's Pier, where they would sit, chat, and unburden on each other about the week. They were the only single ones in their friendship group in Jamaica and their work places were quite close. Kent and Moses, the IT company where she worked, was just a stone's throw away from Byfield and Byfield, the law firm where Camden was a lawyer.

She had excitedly told Camden about the complex, and Camden had been interested. For a few years, he had expressed an interest in leaving his parents' guest house and venturing on his own.

"It's high time, Kenny," he had said, looking at her without his characteristic grin. "I'm ready to make big moves, turn my own key, be the man of my house. Start adulting."

Kenny had laughed.

"I'm not joking, Kenny."

"If you're serious, you should call Richard. He said people were expressing interest in the place before the houses were even finished."

"Tell me more about them," Camden had nodded.

"Three bedrooms, three and a half baths, a large land space, and the view is said to be superb," Kenny said. "Richard used the words premium and luxury. I haven't seen them myself to ascertain what that looks like for him, but he had us design an app for opening the front door remotely and many other cool home automation features."

"Is there yard space for kids to play?" Camden asked.

Kenny had looked at Camden, shocked. "Why?"

"Because I may want a kid or two," Camden said. "I like Rory and Jewel's kid; he's cute and smart."

"That's a given," Kenny said. "Look at his parents. Jewel was reading Algorithms To Live By while she was pregnant with him. She named him Isaac in honor of Isaac Newton."

Camden nodded. "It got me thinking—most of our friends are parents. Maybe I should be looking in that direction. I want a smart kid, too."

"It doesn't work like that," Kenny chuckled. "Besides, don't you need a serious relationship for that to happen? And you're not going to commit until you're forty, remember? You're not even seeing anyone now."

"True, but I have someone in mind," Camden had said mysteriously. "To be honest with you, I've always had her in mind. I wanted to get the wildness out of my system first. I think I'm at the stage where I can present myself to her and say, Hey, I'm serious and ready to be the mature, non-goofy person you've always wanted me to be."

Kenny shook her head. "I can't imagine you being non-goofy. Which girl would want that? You're handsome, but your personality is what's most attractive about you. There is never a dull day with you around."

"Okay, then, I'll be my same old goofy self around her," Camden smiled. "But I'll never be goofy about my feelings."

That was eight months ago; she had never asked him who the mystery girl he had in mind was. She hadn't wanted to seem too interested in his love life. As close as they were, they never really spoke about his various relationships. He was certainly interested in hers, but she usually didn't have much to report. She had one serious relationship, but they broke up around the time she and Camden started hanging out on the weekends.

She looked at him now through the patio doors, holding court in his tastefully furnished luxury home, laughing at a joke and being his adorable, handsome self. For a moment, she slipped. She wished she was by his side, with her hand around his neck, her body pressed to his side, entertaining their guests together.

She turned her back to Camden and looked out at the view. The sea was supposed to be uninteresting at night, but the moon cast a silvery glow over the water, turning it into a shimmering, black glass with sparkles.

She was slipping a lot lately. Camden was her friend, her bestie, her ride-or-die. They had known each other since prep school. In fact, he had been her first crush. For a brief time in high school, they had even considered themselves in a relationship, which had fizzled out almost as soon as it began. They had quarreled about Camden liking the new girl in their third-form class a bit too much.

"I can't be tied down now," Camden had told her in no uncertain terms. "There are so many pretty girls in this school to have relationships with, not just you. I think that having a girlfriend every week would be a perfect solution to my problem."

Kenny had kicked him in the shin and slapped him on the head with her Geography textbook for his little breakup speech.

He had howled with anger. "That's it! We are done! We are no longer boyfriend and girlfriend or even ordinary friends. We will not even talk to each other again!"

Kenny had stomped on his foot for good measure. She knew it would hurt; he had football practice later in the evening, and she wanted him to suffer.

But when she saw that he had left his water bottle in the

classroom after their last class, she had taken it to him at practice.

He had approached her cautiously and taken the bottle from her. "About earlier today, I take it back."

"What are you taking back?" Kenny snarled.

"I'll always be your friend," Camden grinned. "I solemnly swear."

"Save it," Kenny had growled. "You're thirteen years old; you can't solemnly swear anything."

"But I do," Camden corrected her. "And you'll have to swear, too. Solemnly swear that you'll be my friend forever."

"I won't," Kenny had grimaced. "We won't even speak to each other after high school. I'll pass you in the streets in my luxury vehicle and deliberately drive in a puddle so that I can splash you from head to toe."

Camden laughed. "Kenny, you won't always be mad at me. One day, you'll forget all this, and then we'll be friends again. And tell you what, when we are old, we'll try the boyfriend and girlfriend thing again."

"How old are we talking?" Kenny frowned.

"Twenty-six, that seems ancient enough," Camden said. "Give me thirteen more years."

"By twenty-six, I'll be married and have at least two children," Kenny had snickered. "So sorry you'll miss out on all of this." She indicated to her body.

Camden laughed and ran back to his game.

Next month, November, would be her twenty-seventh birthday. She had been so wrong then about her future, but Camden seemed on track with his—except it was not with her. There was the mystery woman—the one who had always been on his mind, the one he was finally ready to pursue. It made her stomach tighten, a feeling she didn't understand and didn't want to explore too deeply. Why was she so reluctant to hear who it was? She didn't know.

Camden was her closest friend at the moment; they told each other everything. He was even closer to her than her girlfriends, Jewel and Audra. Jewel was busy with her young family and rarely had time to do girly stuff these days, and Audra was pursuing her residency at medical school in the States. She only returned to Jamaica for brief visits, and usually, she had her son with her. They couldn't talk about adult stuff with an inquisitive four-year-old constantly around.

Kenny inhaled deeply. She was leaving, back to her lonely apartment, her confused feelings, and her convoluted thoughts about Camden.

She spun around just as Camden was coming onto the patio.

"Kenny, I wondered where you had disappeared to."

"I didn't know you would have noticed I was gone," Kenny said hoarsely. She cleared her throat.

"But of course, I always notice where you are in a room," Camden said ruefully. "It's a habit of mine."

"I was thinking of going home."

"It's early," Camden said, walking closer to her. "And I wanted to say something to you after everybody left."

"I'm not staying behind to help you clean up," Kenny frowned.

Camden chuckled. "I have a housekeeping service for that. I scheduled them to come by at seven tomorrow."

"Oh, well then," Kenny inhaled. "Can we talk tomorrow?"

"Nope," Camden said. "Stay right there. Give me ten minutes, and I'll end this party."

Kenny nodded. "Okay."

It took him closer to twenty minutes.

Kenny had stretched out on the lounger and closed her

eyes when she felt him beside her.

"Scoot over," Camden said.

She moved over, and he sank down beside her.

"You smell so good," Kenny inhaled. "Has anybody ever told you that you wear the best colognes?"

Camden chuckled. "I hear that all the time, thanks to you. You buy my colognes."

"So, what do you want to talk about?" Kenny asked.

"Do you ever think about the future?" Camden asked, his tone unusually serious.

Kenny nodded. Their faces were close to each other. "Sometimes. I mean, who doesn't?"

"I'm not talking about just any future. I'm talking about... our future."

"Our future?" Kenny's heart skipped a beat. What was he getting at?

Camden caressed her cheek. "We've been friends for so long, and I've been thinking... maybe it's time we tried something more."

The words hung in the air, heavy and unexpected. Kenny stared at him, her mind racing. She was his mystery girl?

"I can't keep pretending I don't feel something more for you than friendship," Camden whispered. "I've been falling for you for a long time, and I'm ready to see where this could go."

Kenny looked into his eyes, searching for any hint of the old Camden she knew—the one who always had a joke ready and was never serious about anything except his work. But all she saw was sincerity. And maybe, just maybe, that was what scared her the most.

"I don't know what to say," she whispered. "I thought you were going to tell me about your mystery girl."

"The mystery girl is you," Camden said. "I've been giving

you broad hints about my changing feelings and intentions for months, and you've ignored them."

"But..." Kenny whispered.

"We've been hanging out for the past year, spending every moment together," Camden said. "I hated going home without you after our Friday night dates. I think you should move in with me."

"Move in?" Kenny chuckled. "We've never even kissed."

Camden pulled her toward him and placed his lips on hers.

Kenny froze momentarily, her mind racing to catch up with the sudden shift in their relationship. But as Camden's lips moved gently against hers, all her doubts began to melt away. She felt a warmth spreading through her, a sense of rightness she didn't expect. She leaned into the kiss, letting herself fall into the moment.

When they finally pulled apart, they were breathing heavily.

"Wow," Kenny murmured. "I had no idea you were such a good kisser."

"If you move in with me, we'll kiss every day. I'll get to be an even better kisser," Camden murmured.

"Okay," she whispered, her voice trembling slightly. "I'll do it. No, what am I saying? My mother will have a heart attack over this. There's no proposal here..."

"I'll propose," Camden said, "but only after we've lived together for two years. Then, we'll assess the state of our relationship. Those are the terms. Will you agree to them?"

Chapter Two

Present Day

It was Wednesday, and Kenny did not want to get out of bed. It was raining and she could see the raindrops against the patio door. She snuggled closer to Camden in a spooning position.

"I have to go in early today," Camden said sleepily.

"Me too," Kenny murmured. "Team meeting, big account."

Camden wrapped his arm around her and pulled her closer. "Same thing with us. We have an interesting case going on at the moment. Dad wants all hands on deck—even Grandad is coming out of retirement for it. This could be my chance to outshine the cousins. The position for junior partner is up for grabs. My dad and Uncle Noel are making it obvious that this year if we snooze, we lose."

Kenny chuckled. There is heavy competition at the Byfield and Byfield law firm these days. It was a family practice set up by William and Richard Byfield in the fifties. Their sons, Noel and Jim, had taken over and expanded the outfit, and now their children—Camden, Alan, and Ashton—were gunning for a junior partner position. It wasn't just an automatic assignment because their last name was Byfield.

They had strict protocols to follow and a rigorous evaluation process that left no room for favoritism. Camden had been working tirelessly for months, trying to outshine his cousins, each of whom had their own strengths and connections within the firm. Alan was known for his razor-sharp legal mind and ability to dissect a case down to the tiniest detail, while Ashton had a knack for charming clients and winning them over with his persuasive arguments.

Camden, however, had something they didn't—an instinctive understanding of people, a way of reading between the lines that often led him to solutions others missed. His grandfather, Richard, had always said that Camden had the 'Byfield intuition,' a trait that couldn't be taught but was invaluable in the practice.

"You'll knock it out of the park," Kenny said, her voice muffled against his chest. "Just remember to use your Byfield intuition. That's what sets you apart."

Camden smiled and kissed the top of her head. "Thanks, babe. I'll need all the luck I can get."

Kenny sighed, still reluctant to leave the warmth of their bed. "What's the big case you guys are working on?"

"It's a family dispute over huge swaths of land," Camden murmured. "The family patriarch, Kingsley Hart, just died. He left it equally to his sons, Aiden and Blake Hart. They can't agree on what to do with the property. They hate each other's guts and can't agree on anything, so no surprise there. But it's a doozy of a case. A cousin has come out of the woodwork claiming he's also an heir and has video evidence to prove it. You'll no doubt hear more about it in the weeks to come."

"Wait a minute," Kenny said. "I know the name Hart, as in the Hartland group of companies."

"That's right," Camden said.

"Didn't both brothers marry the same woman at different times? And she had one set of children for the older brother and another set for the younger brother?" Kenny asked.

"Right again," Camden murmured.

"And then one of the brothers killed her?" Kenny got up and stretched.

"Don't know about that—it's all speculation," Camden yawned. "Why do you have to get up? We have five minutes left. We could squeeze in a quickie."

"Nope," Kenny wagged her finger at him. "Later. I don't want to be late for this meeting. And we never manage to have a quickie. It's always the opposite of a quickie."

"That's because I have to take my time with you," Camden grinned boyishly.

Kenny smiled, her heart melting a little. "You are truly outstanding in the bedroom, that I can't deny. But I'm a team leader now; I have to set an example. And I don't want to risk being late to a meeting with the bosses, Kent and Moses."

Camden nodded. "Don't forget the Cycle Club get-together tonight. It's at Howie's Pub."

"Do I have to go?" Kenny grumbled. "I sincerely believe Jody throws these meetings and launches just so she can meet and plan things with you. It's never that serious."

Camden chuckled. "She does like to meet, doesn't she?"

"Yes," Kenny said, "she made you de facto president so she could keep you close to her. And don't deny it. That girl has been into you for years. She doesn't disguise her attraction to you one bit. Why haven't you ever dated her? She certainly sends out a lot of hints that she'd just die if you did."

"I've never seen her that way," Camden murmured. "There are some women who just don't do it for me. I guess she's one of them."

Kenny raised a brow. "I wonder why Jody doesn't do it for you."

"I don't know," Camden frowned. "I just never thought of her that way. Well, that's not true. About three years ago, I lightly toyed with the idea when I started going to her for hamstring pain, and then you and I started hanging out, and that was it."

"Really?" Kenny grinned. "Tall, lean, and modelesque Jody was pushed aside for little old me?"

"Yup," Camden nodded.

"But you dated everyone in your vicinity who fit her profile," Kenny said, baffled.

"No, I haven't," Camden grimaced. "I hate this perception you have of me in your head. I was a player only briefly while I was at university. I got it all out of my system. I find that I'm much better off being in a relationship with you. I love it this way."

Kenny smiled. She loved it when Camden said things like that.

"And that's why I think you should come to the event tonight," Camden said. "I'm the president, you're my first lady, and we're launching our charity event for the year. I need you by my side as we present a united front to our citizens—including Jody."

Kenny chuckled. "What's the charity event for?"

"The Heart Foundation," Camden said. "Jody was the one who chose the charity, arranged the party, and forced me to show up. You should've gotten an email with this year's itinerary."

"I did," Kenny looked at him aghast. "I totally forgot about it. I read the emails; I really do. I must've missed that one. I guess I'm a terrible member of the Cycling Club."

"And so am I," Camden said. "If it weren't for Jody nominating me as president, I wouldn't be in this pickle. I was quite fine being an ordinary member, showing up for our Sunday morning rides, and having fun. Now I have to okay things like charity events, monitor expenses, and do all these presidential things. I'll be so happy to hand it off to some other sucker next year."

"I loved our Sunday morning rides," Kenny said as she got up. "I haven't done one of those in months. Remember when we rode from Montego Bay to Kingston and then back?"

"Yup." Camden nodded. "Not doing that again. My groin still aches thinking about it."

"It was fun," Kenny grinned.

She headed for the bathroom, pulling off her hair bonnet and staring at herself in the mirror. She looked good. Her face had inexplicably broken out into fine bumps a few weeks ago, and it had gotten so alarming she'd gone to the doctor.

"Change your birth control," he had said matter-of-factly, and she had. Now her skin was picture-perfect. Her smooth peanut butter skin tone showed nary a blemish or rash. Her eyes were clear, and her smile was bright and even after finally removing her retainers a couple of months ago. She tilted her head to the side, admiring how her hair framed her face.

It was growing unbelievably fast. The old birth control had probably messed with her hair growth cycle because she hadn't seen her hair this long since... ever. Three years ago, she had followed her sister Kendrea to a hairdresser for her big chop and ended up getting one herself.

After the first year of wrestling with it, she found that mini-twisting her own hair was her favorite style. It was versatile and fuss-free, and her hair was longer than it had ever been. She retwisted it every month, and it was due for a retwist.

Last night, she plaited it in big chunks so the twists could be curly today. She would wear it down. It was long—almost mid-back—and looked lush, springy, and thick. That hairstyle, paired with her black pantsuit and white shirt, would transition nicely to the get-together tonight.

Kenny had to admit she looked better heading into her thirties than she had as a teenager. She had a glow, a confidence that came from knowing herself better and embracing who she truly was. The insecurities of her younger years had faded, replaced by a quiet self-assurance.

She was about to turn away from her reflection when she spotted a grey hair.

She moved closer to the mirror and squealed. This wouldn't do—she was still in her twenties! She hunted for the scissors. She was going to cut it out.

"What are you doing?" Camden asked from the bathroom door. "What's taking so long?"

"I have a grey hair!" Kenny looked at him, stricken. "I'm going to cut it out."

Camden laughed. "Leave it, I like it."

"How can you like it?" Kenny fretted. "They're going to take over. This is the beginning of the end!"

"I like everything about you," Camden said, kissing her on the neck. "Stop being vain, Kenny. Accept your grey hairs gracefully and go shower, or I'm going to shower before you."

"How is it that I have a grey hair before you?" Kenny looked at him curiously. "I'm going to dye it."

"Wait until you have a fistful," Camden said. "It's just one grey hair. There's no need to be self-conscious about it. Besides, I think the whole grey hair look will suit you. Maybe you'll be lucky, and only one side of your head will turn grey. Now that would be something—a lovely style statement."

Kenny rolled her eyes but couldn't help the small smile tugging at her lips. "You would say that," she muttered, still eyeing the offending strand in the mirror.

Camden chuckled and wrapped his arms around her from bchind, resting his chin on her shoulder. "You're beautiful, Kenny, with or without grey hairs. They just add a little character, a little wisdom."

She leaned back into him, feeling the warmth of his embrace. "You're just saying that to make me feel better."

"I'm saying it because it's true," he replied, pressing a kiss to her temple. "Besides, one grey hair doesn't change who you are or how stunning you look. It's just a reminder that we're all getting a little older—and hopefully a little wiser, too."

Kenny sighed, her initial panic fading as she considered his words. He had a way of grounding her, of reminding her what truly mattered. "Fine, I won't cut it. But if I find any more, I'm not promising anything."

"Deal," Camden grinned, releasing her. "Now, go finish getting ready before we're late."

She gave him a playful shove toward the door. "Alright, alright. I'm going."

Chapter Three

Howie's Pub was a rustic meeting place near the sea. The pub owner, Howard Lewis—who answered to Howie—was an expat from Britain, eager to create a traditional pub atmosphere with a Caribbean twist. The Pub was large, with wide wooden beams crisscrossing the ceiling and walls adorned with various cycling memorabilia.

The scent of saltwater mingled with the rich aroma of grilled seafood, filling the air. Howie had gone to great lengths to blend British charm with the laid-back vibe of the islands. Wooden tables and chairs, worn smooth by years of use, were scattered throughout the Pub, offering plenty of space for locals and tourists alike. A long bar made from polished mahogany stretched across one side of the room, stocked with an impressive selection of British ales and Caribbean rum.

Outside, a spacious deck overlooked the sparkling ocean, where guests could enjoy their drinks while listening to the waves crashing against the shore. At night, the deck was lit with soft lanterns, casting a warm glow over the sea and adding to the Pub's cozy, inviting atmosphere.

A small stage in the corner often hosts live music from local bands playing a mix of calypso and reggae, giving the Pub a lively yet relaxed energy. There was no live band or patrons tonight, just the cycling club members milling around and chatting. Howie had been the one to start that chapter of the cycling club. The first meetings had been held at the Pub, and it had continued that way for twelve years since its inception.

The original seven-member group had grown to nearly seventy. Camden had been the one to introduce Kenny to the lively group of like-minded cycling enthusiasts.

Kenny's only familiarity with a bicycle had been a tricycle her father bought her when she was five. She had outgrown that, and her younger sister, Kennice, had inherited it. So when Camden suggested she join the club, she had initially balked at the idea. But she was so glad she had done it. It provided exercise and good fun at the same time. Plus, she had met many amazing people and ridden the scenic routes of Jamaica.

"Kenny!" Howie beckoned to her from behind the bar as soon as she entered.

He was lean and fit, a little over fifty, and so tanned that they were almost the same complexion. His blue eyes sparkled as he leaned forward. "I have a favor to ask. I know you build apps, right?"

"Right," Kenny nodded.

"Can you build one for us?"

"What sort of app are you thinking of?" Kenny asked.

"Just a basic cycling app specific to us," Howie said, rubbing his chin. "I imagine it would include routes, meeting points, and event schedules. Maybe even a feature where members can log their rides and track their progress over time. It doesn't have to be anything fancy—just something that keeps us all connected and informed. You know how some of the older members aren't too tech-savvy, so it needs to be simple and user-friendly."

Kenny smiled, considering the idea. "That sounds doable. I could integrate GPS to map out routes, add a calendar for events, and maybe even a chat feature for members to communicate. A leaderboard might be fun too—see who's clocking the most miles each week. However, I don't have the time, Howie. Today at work, we got a huge project to tackle."

Howie looked disappointed. "Well, that's a bummer."

"Tell you what," Kenny said, "I'll try to tackle it on the weekends when I'm free. How's that?"

"Brilliant!" Howie smiled, showing his slightly crooked teeth.

"Howie, can you help me?" Jody asked briskly from behind them. "I want to put the banner with the theme over there." She pointed to a corner wall. "I figure it'll be the perfect place for our group pictures, which I'm sure will be in the papers for promotional purposes. I invited a reporter to tonight's meeting."

Howie nodded and took the banner from Jody.

Kenny read the banner. It said: *Ride or Die*. She just knew Camden had come up with the slogan—he liked to call her his ride or die.

Jody turned to Kenny. "Oh, hi, Kenny, or should I say, stranger. You haven't been to a meeting or one of our Sunday rides in months."

"I know. I've been super busy," Kenny said.

"That's okay," Jody replied. "I imagine you didn't want to

come around since your breakup with Camden."

"I haven't broken up with Camden," Kenny frowned. "We're still going strong."

"Still?" Jody's eyes widened.

"Why, what did you hear?" Kenny asked suspiciously.

Jody laughed, a bit self-consciously. "Nothing. Forgive my big mouth. It's just that I know Camden, and he's not the type to stay with a girl for long. I just assumed you two were over."

"We live together," Kenny said. "Camden and I are committed to each other."

"I was wondering how long that arrangement would last," Jody smirked. "But living together is not marriage, so anything could happen."

Kenny inhaled deeply. How many times had she told herself that? Especially as the two-year deadline for them to assess their relationship approached, and Camden hadn't brought it up.

Jody looked at her slyly, sensing she had touched a nerve. "At the end of the day, he can just walk away."

"Or I could walk away," Kenny pointed out. "Why are you assuming Camden is the prize?"

"Because he is," Jody shrugged. "Men like him are rare. He's from a good family, has a professional career, owns his house, has a nice personality, is considerate, and is so handsome."

"He looks like a model straight out of a magazine," Jody continued, her tone almost envious. "Tall, athletic build, with deep brown skin that's smooth and flawless. His jawline is sharp, perfectly complementing his high cheekbones. And those eyes—dark and intense, like he's always thinking about something profound. He's got that kind of smile that lights up a room, and there's something about the way he carries himself—confident but not arrogant—that makes him impossible to ignore. Girl, I would not be so blasé about him. I would lock him down in matrimony if I were you."

"Maybe we're not ready," Kenny said weakly.

"Not ready?" Jody raised her eyebrows. "Why not? Is he a pain to live with?"

"No," Kenny said slowly, wondering why she was telling this woman her business. Jody had hit a nerve, and the way she described Camden almost reverently made Kenny want to walk away from the conversation.

"That's what I thought," Jody said. "I've watched Camden over the years—he has great qualities. My mother would say he's husband material. He's probably the neatest man I know. He hates clutter."

"Yep," Kenny nodded. "Camden is neat, washes up after himself, takes out the garbage without being asked—he's easy to live with."

"Ooh, someone's going to snatch that man away," Jody said. "You're skating on thin ice, Kenny. My sister was in your shoes. She lived with someone for three years, and when she started hinting that she wanted more, he left her for a cousin of ours who was visiting from the States. They got married six weeks after he left my poor sister."

"They're still together and happy. My mother talks to our cousin frequently, and she's always boasting about how easy he is to live with—how attentive he is with small things like taking out the trash, squeezing the toothpaste from the bottom, putting away his junk, and not cluttering the place. My sister taught him all of that. She made him into the perfect husband... for someone else."

Kenny cleared her throat. "Jody…"

"You know the lessons I learned from all of this, Kenny?" Jody asked.

Kenny shook her head. "I'm sure you're going to tell me."

"Lesson one: When you live with a guy without the benefit of marriage, technically, he's still single and fair game to every woman—including women in your own family. Lesson two: Don't be the sucker who prepares a man to be the perfect husband for another woman. And lesson three: Living with a guy means you're not solid. Make him commit, or just quit."

Kenny looked at her, aghast. "Thanks for the advice, but Camden and I are fine for now."

Jody laughed and then leaned closer. "You think you're different—that Camden won't ever leave—but people change, Kenny. Circumstances change. And if you think you can keep playing house without any real security, you're fooling yourself."

Kenny felt her pulse quicken. Jody's words were striking deeper than she expected. Was she really being foolish? Was her relationship as solid as she believed? She opened her mouth to defend Camden, to argue that their love was enough, but the words caught in her throat.

Jody looked at her knowingly. "In the meantime, don't trust any woman around him, including me. Especially me. I don't mess with married men, but if there is no ring, girl, I'm going to pounce. Give me an inch, and I'll take a mile."

She cackled with laughter and then glanced in Howie's direction. "Excuse me, Kenny, but Howie isn't hanging that banner right. I need to supervise."

And just like that, she was gone, leaving Kenny with the unsettling echo of her words. Jody's bluntness had hit her like a cold splash of water, jolting her out of the comfortable haze she'd been living in.

It wasn't that she didn't trust Camden—she did. But Jody had planted a seed of doubt, a nagging voice in the back of her mind that wouldn't be easily silenced. It had been two years, three months, and four days since she moved in with him. They were supposed to have discussed their status after two years. She hadn't wanted to bring it up because she thought Camden would bring it up first.

Kenny stood there, feeling a mix of emotions she couldn't quite name. She wanted to dismiss Jody's warnings, but the truth was, there was a logic to what Jody had said that Kenny couldn't ignore.

She looked around the room, her eyes landing on Camden, who had just entered the Pub. Already, he was swarmed by people vying for his attention—Mr. Life of the Party, forever the people magnet.

He caught her gaze and smiled warmly, the kind of smile that always made her feel secure and loved. But now, a shadow of doubt lingered behind her own smile as she tried to push away the questions Jody's words had stirred up.

Was she really doing enough to secure her future with Camden? Or was she just floating along, hoping for the best without any real plan? They had agreed on a time to assess their relationship, and she had blithely ignored it.

The thought unnerved her, and as she watched Camden, she couldn't help but wonder if he was as committed as she believed—or if he, too, was just enjoying the ride without considering where it was going.

Kenny sighed, turning away from the lively scene around her and heading to the patio, where it was quieter. Maybe it was time for a real conversation with Camden, where they could both lay their cards on the table.

She needed to know if they were on the same page or if Jody's cynical view of their relationship had a point. The last thing she wanted was to wake up one day and find that she had been preparing Camden for someone else's happily ever after.

Chapter Four

Unfortunately, they didn't get to have their deep talk that night. They had driven separate cars to the event, and as soon as they got home, Camden was roped into a conference call with some other lawyers about the Hartland case.

That call had lasted well into the night. She was half-asleep when he finally got into bed and snuggled against her, and he was still asleep when she got up in the morning, even though she banged around a little to make him wake up.

Now, here she was in the cafeteria, studiously separating her salad into little mounds, unaware that Jewel had slipped into the seat across from her.

"What on earth has you so preoccupied?" Jewel asked.

Kenny looked up at her friend, who, as usual, was effortlessly pretty. Even dressed in standard business wear with not a lick of makeup, Jewel was still fascinating to look at.

"Stop staring and start talking," Jewel said, pulling out her lunch from her bag and opening up containers.

"Oh my," Kenny murmured. "That looks delicious."

"Jill made it, leftovers from Lily's birthday party." Jewel smiled. "Want to share?"

"Of course, I want to share," Kenny said, licking her lips. "I just made a simple salad. I had no idea Jill threw a party for her daughter. Why wasn't I invited?"

"I'm sure she would've invited you if you had a kid," Jewel said. "It was a kid's party."

Kenny sighed. "Oh yes, I keep getting left out more and more from the exclusive mommy club. You guys have your little gatherings, talk mommy talk, and reminisce about how hard parenting is while I'm left out in the cold—single, unmarried, and childless."

"Ah," Jewel nodded. "So that's why you're looking so spaced out—you haven't had the two-year talk with Camden."

"Two years, three months, and five days," Kenny corrected. "He hasn't brought up the marriage conversation. Should I bring it up first?"

"Yes," Jewel nodded.

"I don't want to seem needy. I don't want to be a bother," Kenny muttered. "If he wanted to get married, he would've said something. I'm going to push things, and we're going to break up. I can feel it."

"Whoa," Jewel said. "I thought you were happy with Camden."

"We are happy. It's working, we jive, it's easy," Kenny said. "And that's why I'm reluctant to upset the applecart."

"Then don't upset it," Jewel said.

"How can you say that?" Kenny asked. "You got married while still in college. You didn't even wait long, and you and Rory are still going strong. I'm twenty-nine years old, Jewel. This is not how I wanted my life to turn out. I don't want to be the girl sending out broad hints to the guy I live with, begging for a wedding ring. And I definitely don't want to be the girl who, after house-training her man, watches him leave for someone else and marry her after six weeks."

"That's weirdly specific," Jewel frowned. "Whose situation is that?"

"Jody's sister," Kenny sighed. "I had a talk with Jody last night, and I guess I'm still unsettled by it."

"Ah," Jewel nodded. "Little Miss Jody doing her part to derail your relationship. Jody's made no secret of the fact that she has the hots for Camden. I would take anything she says with a grain of salt."

"She made a good point, though," Kenny said. "She said as long as Camden and I aren't married, he's fair game—especially to her."

"If a man is going to cheat, he'll cheat whether you're married or not," Jewel replied. "And women like Jody will pursue them regardless of a ring. I think it's up to both you and Camden to stick to your commitment to each other, whether you're married or not. That said, I think you should have a frank, honest conversation with him about your two-year assessment. He's probably so comfortable with the situation that he's not going to be the one to bring it up. You'll have to do it."

Kenny sighed. "If I were prettier, I wouldn't have to grovel for marriage. My sister Kendrea gets proposed to at least once a week, you got married in no time, your sister-in-law Shay was practically hounded to the altar by Jeremiah, my dad married my mom when they were fresh out of high school, and my stepfather proposed to my mom a week after they started dating. And here I am, waiting two years, which could turn into twenty. I'm not waiting twenty years for a proposal."

Jewel chuckled. "You are pretty, and you know it. And in all those situations you mentioned, nobody got married—or stayed married—just based on looks. You have a good thing going with Camden. Do what you always do: communicate. Ask him about the two-year deadline."

Kenny nodded. "Okay. I hear you."

"You don't sound like you're going to do it," Jewel frowned.

"I am," Kenny inhaled. "I am. It's just that it feels like the worst time for us to have this conversation. Camden's working on a big case and jockeying for a partnership over his cousins."

Jewel nodded. "I see."

"I know what you're thinking," Kenny said. "You're thinking there's always going to be something, and I'm being foolish for putting it off."

"Girl, quit your job now and go start up a psychic hotline," Jewel grinned. "It's like you dragged that thought straight from my mind."

Kenny picked up her phone. "Okay, already. I will text him and invite him to dinner at our favorite spot near the house. We'll get a quiet table on the patio, and then we'll talk."

"Good," Jewel nodded.

Kenny texted Camden and then whistled. "Look at that— Audra just texted me. Her parents urged her to come home and join their practice, and she finally said yes. She'll complete the move back home in two weeks."

Jewel chuckled. "I thought Audra would never return to Jamaica because her mysterious baby daddy is out here."

"I don't think he is, though," Kenny said. "But what do I

know? She's never told me who he is."

Jewel chuckled. "Eight years later, and we're still speculating about Audra's baby daddy. We're poor detectives."

Kenny chuckled. "True. But we don't have many facts to work with. She wasn't in a relationship when she got pregnant, she never talked about anyone, blindsided us with the pregnancy, quit medical school, moved to America, and hasn't brought up the paternity question even once—despite my much hinting and probing. Last year, when she came back with Jason, I found myself searching the little boy's face for clues."

"Rory and I were doing the same thing," Jewel nodded. "If only Audra would give us a hint."

"Jason doesn't look like her," Kenny said, "not even a little bit. He doesn't look like anyone in her family. And I know all of Audra's family."

"Maybe we'll never know," Jewel shrugged. "But that's fine. I'm just happy she picked up her medical degree again and specialized in pediatrics. We need more pediatricians on this side of the island."

Kenny nodded. "So enough about Audra. How are your mom and Phillip?"

"Great," Jewel said. "My mom's pregnant with twins. Any day now, she's going to pop."

Kenny giggled. "I always get a kick out of hearing that your mom is Pearl Day and her husband is Phillip Knight."

Jewel grinned. "She gets a kick out of it too. She's been planning some outlandish names like Moon Knight and Sunny Knight. Say a prayer for my brother and sister."

"A boy and a girl," Kenny said wistfully. "That must be nice."

"I didn't even know you were ready for kids," Jewel

looked at her in amazement. "You sound positively broody. What's changed?"

"Maybe I am ready for kids," Kenny said. "You have one, Audra has one. Camden and I used to talk about it all the time, and I wasn't the one who was ready. Now, I think maybe I am."

"One more topic for you to bring up at dinner tonight," Jewel said. "I wish you all the best."

****

"**D**inner at Bay View," Kenny texted him. "Is seven o'clock okay?"

Camden groaned. It was Friday night, their standard date night, and yes, he would love to go to dinner, but at the rate his grandfather was talking at the head of the table in the conference room, he felt as if he wouldn't leave the meeting until next week. The man took his time with his words.

He surreptitiously texted back: "I'm in a meeting. I'll call you as soon as I'm done to confirm. No, scrap that. I'm game if my grandfather ever stops speaking."

He stifled a yawn; his grandfather was speaking as if he were choosing his words carefully and deliberately. Where was a fast-forward button in real life when you needed one?

He glanced across at his cousin Alan, who looked weary—an unusual sight, as he usually knew how to fake attentiveness quite well. His other cousin, Ashton, had closed his eyes; it was hard to tell if he was sleeping.

Camden wanted to leave so badly, but he couldn't, with his competition still present and under the keen watchful eyes of his father and uncle. All three of them would eventually become partners in the law firm anyway; only Byfields could be partners. The non-family lawyers were associates.

The only reason for the competition between him and his cousins was the rule that allowed only one junior partner to be named each year. The first of the three to be named this year could forever boast that they got it first, that the senior partners saw potential in them, and that the family trusted them to lead. It was a matter of pride and legacy, not just a title.

Securing the junior partner position this year would solidify Camden's standing in the family and the firm, setting the tone for the rest of his career. But right now, all he could think about was getting out of this meeting and spending the evening with Kenny. The thought of Bay View's cozy ambiance and Kenny's infectious laughter was the only thing keeping him from nodding off.

His grandfather's voice droned on, discussing some intricate point of law that Camden was sure had been covered before, but the old man liked to be thorough. Camden's phone buzzed again—another text from Kenny.

"I know you're probably bored out of your mind. Just let me know when you're free."

Camden allowed himself a small smile. Kenny knew him too well. He quickly typed a response: "You have no idea. I'll do my best to make it. Can't wait to see you."

As he hit send, his grandfather finally paused, looking at the three of them with a knowing glint in his eye. "Remember, boys," the old man said, "this firm isn't just about winning cases. It's about upholding the family's reputation. We've built this over generations, and it's your responsibility to carry it forward."

The meeting dragged on for another half hour, with his grandfather wrapping up with a reminder of the upcoming junior partner selection and the importance of unity within the family. As they were dismissed, Camden's father caught his eye and gave him a subtle nod, a silent acknowledgment of the work ahead.

Camden gathered his things, shooting a quick glance at his cousins, both of whom seemed relieved to be free. As they filed out of the conference room, Alan muttered something about needing a drink.

"I am going home to shower and then I'm hitting up Mingles. What are you doing, Camden?"

"Dinner with Kenny," Camden said. "It's date night."

"Tell me something," Ashton's eyes lit up. "Are any of Kenny's sisters single? If any of them are as hot as Kenny, I could set myself up with the same situation you're enjoying."

Camden chuckled. "Two of them are married; one is single, I think."

"You think?" Ashton raised an eyebrow.

"I don't know," Camden shrugged. "One never knows with Kendrea. She's super private about her love life."

Ashton was on a perpetual girl hunt and seemed to attract the wrong types.

"Hey, good luck tonight," Camden said. "I'm running late."

"Okay, have fun," Ashton nodded.

Camden checked his phone again. There were no new messages, but it was almost seven. He quickly dialed Kenny's number as he headed for the elevator.

"Hey," Kenny's voice came through, warm and familiar.

"Hey," Camden replied, finally feeling the tension of the day start to ease. "I'm on my way. Bay View in thirty?"

"Perfect," Kenny said, and Camden could hear the smile in her voice. "I'll be waiting."

Chapter Five

Kenny was nervous about something. They were seated at their favorite table on the patio at the Bay View Restaurant; it was the perfect place for intimate conversation and good food after a long week's work. Soothing R&B music played in the background. Currently, Anita Baker was singing It's Been You All the Time. "Like somebody turned on a light. It took just a minute, but now that I'm in it, it's you…"

He felt a sense of déjà vu. This was the exact song playing nearly three years ago when he and Kenny had met up here, and he had the brilliant idea that he couldn't live without her. Like the song said, it was like somebody had turned on a light in his head. And though he hadn't realized it—or was unwilling to admit it even to himself—it had always been Kenny for him. Through the years, even when they had just been friends, they had always found a way to be in each other's lives, like two puzzle pieces that just fit together naturally.

It wasn't until that night three years ago that Camden finally understood what had been right in front of him all along. The connection they shared was more than just friendship—it was something deeper. He wanted her in his life so badly that he almost frightened himself with the intensity of how much he wanted it.

"So, what are we doing this weekend?" Kenny asked.

"Nothing," Camden said. "Absolutely zero. I just want to be. This is the calm before a stormy couple of weeks ahead, and I want to get my zen in before the craziness starts at work and the Cycle Club charity event."

"And my mom and stepdad's anniversary dinner."

Camden nodded. "And that. You do realize you have a family event every month, don't you?"

Kenny nodded. "It's a side effect of having so many siblings and stepsiblings. Small families can't relate."

"And we don't want to," Camden chuckled. "It's just me and my sister and the occasional family gathering with the extended family. Our kids will be overwhelmed."

Kenny cleared her throat. "Our kids?"

"Well, yes," Camden said. "We want to have at least two, don't we?"

Kenny nodded. "Yes, when we are married. And speaking of marriage, the two years for reassessment are up. Shouldn't we be discussing that?"

Camden sighed and leaned back in his chair. He had realized that the two years were up; he just didn't want to rush into something that was too important to get wrong. The timing had always been tricky for them—both were busy with their careers, social obligations, and personal goals. But he knew Kenny wasn't just another part of his life; she was the most significant part.

"Yeah, I've been thinking about it a lot," Camden admitted,

his eyes meeting hers. "But I want to make sure we're both ready. I don't want to make promises I can't keep or rush into something because of a deadline we set two years ago."

Kenny glared at him. "Two years is not rushing. I need to know that we're moving forward, Camden. That we're not just standing still, waiting for the perfect time that might never come."

"I get that. I do. And I want this too, more than anything. But marriage is… it's big. It's forever. And I don't want what we have to fail after getting married. What I'm trying to say is, we have a good thing going on now; marriage might wreck it."

"How?" Kenny asked him.

Camden ran a hand through his hair, trying to find the right words. "Because marriage changes things," he began. "It's not just a piece of paper or a ring. It's a commitment to be with someone through everything, good and bad. And I'm not saying I don't want that with you—I do. But I've seen people rush into marriage and then fall apart because they weren't ready for what it really meant. I don't want us to become one of those couples who thought love was enough to keep things going."

Kenny's expression softened slightly, but her eyes still held that determined glint. "I'm not asking for a fairy tale, Camden. I know marriage is hard work. I know it's not always going to be perfect, but I also know that I'm ready to take that step with you. We've built something solid over these past few years—something worth fighting for. But I need to know that we're heading in the same direction and want to take that next step together."

Camden nodded slowly, absorbing her words. "I guess I'm just scared. Scared of failing you, of not being the husband you deserve."

"You won't fail me," Kenny said. "We've made it through so much already, and if there's one thing I'm sure of, it's that we're better together than apart. We are each other's ride or die, remember?"

Camden took a deep breath. He knew she was right—they had weathered storms before and always came out stronger. But to make that final commitment was still a little daunting in his head. How was he like this?

Because of his parents, of course. They were together for nearly forty years but didn't have a traditional marriage. He had unfortunately found that out when he was ten, after walking in on an orgy in the pool house with his parents and another couple. They had been suitably horrified that he had found out. They had even sent him to counseling, but what he couldn't reconcile in his brain, even after adulthood, was how his parents could maintain such a strong facade of love and unity while engaging in something that seemed to contradict everything he believed marriage should be.

It was confusing for him as a child, and even now, as an adult, the memory haunted him. How could two people be so committed to each other yet seek something unconventional outside their marriage? It made him question the very foundation of what a committed relationship was supposed to be.

His parents had always told him that love was about trust, about letting the other person be who they were without judgment. But what they didn't realize was that their version of trust had shattered his understanding of fidelity, of what it meant to truly be with someone. His idea of marriage was completely warped.

After living with Kenny for two years, he realized that a normal marriage could be possible, but he was still a tiny bit reluctant to take the final plunge. Of course, he could explain all of this to Kenny, but he had never told anyone about his parents. He didn't even think his sister knew; she was five years younger than he was and had never been exposed to that side of them. He was reluctant to shatter her illusions.

To give his parents credit, they never brought their sexual escapades home again. They went away at least once a month on a weekend getaway with their 'friends.' His sister thought it was cute how tight-knit they and their friends were, while Camden wished he didn't know what exactly that was about.

It was a wonder he wasn't more messed up. His parents and their friends projected an image to the world that seemed perfect from the outside, but Camden knew better. He knew the truth behind those smiles and dinner parties, the hidden layers of their relationships that no one else saw. It had left him with a deep mistrust of anything that seemed too perfect, too polished. He'd always been skeptical of relationships, always waiting for the other shoe to drop, for the hidden flaws to reveal themselves.

That's why his relationship with Kenny was both comforting and terrifying. With her, there were no secrets, no masks. What they had was real, built on honesty and mutual respect. But even though he knew Kenny wasn't like his parents, that she valued commitment and fidelity just as much as he did, he couldn't completely shake the fear that something might go wrong if they took that final step into marriage.

Camden often wondered if he should tell Kenny the truth about his parents and why he hesitated when it came to marriage. But every time he considered it, the words stuck in his throat. He didn't want to burden her with his past or risk tainting what they had by bringing up something so dark and complicated. Kenny had her own dreams of what their marriage would look like, and he didn't want to cast a shadow over that.

Yet, he also knew that keeping this part of himself hidden was a form of dishonesty, a crack in the foundation they were trying to build. If he truly wanted to move forward with Kenny and be the husband she deserved, he had to confront his past, even if it meant opening up about the things that still haunted him.

Camden sighed, running a hand through his hair as he looked at Kenny, who was watching him with concern in her eyes. He knew he couldn't keep avoiding the issue, couldn't keep hiding behind his fears. If they were going to build a life together, it had to be on a foundation of complete trust.

But he wasn't ready.

"I guess what I'm trying to say," Camden began, his voice steadying, "is that I'm in. All in. I want to marry you, Kenny. I want to have those kids we talked about and build a life with you. But I need to know we're doing it for the right reasons—not because of some deadline, but because we both feel it's time. Maybe we should do another assessment in two more years. Besides, we don't need a wedding ring to confirm that what we have is solid."

"Listen to me," Kenny leaned in closer, her voice soft but firm. "We've been together for a while; there is no further assessment to make. I am not going to stick around for two more years to find out something that I knew all along. I know it's the fashionable thing to do these days, but I don't want to be a baby mother."

"You're not pregnant, are you?" Camden asked.

"No," Kenny said, "but I wouldn't mind starting a family before I'm thirty. And if we delay two more years, I'm going to be thirty-one. And then, seeing this trajectory that we seem to be on, I'll be thirty-three if we do another assessment in two more years. Two more years after that, I'll be thirty-five.

"You see where I'm going with this, Camden? By the time you look around, I can't have kids anymore. And I don't want to get married just because I am pregnant. I want you to marry me for me because we are good together. No other reason."

"Where is all of this coming from?" Camden asked.

"I spoke to Jody at the charity launch the other night," Kenny said. "She mocked me for living with you without commitment and said that because of that, we were single and technically fair game."

"I should have known she was behind this," Camden muttered. "Jody doesn't know when to butt out of people's business."

"But she was right, though, Camden," Kenny said. "Who's to say you won't find somebody else and marry them in six weeks? While I am sitting here waiting for a two-year assessment like a chump. If we don't sort this out in a month, I am moving out."

Camden stared at Kenny in astonishment. "This is blackmail."

"No, it's not," Kenny said. "It's an ultimatum. Marriage or I am bolting."

"Kenny, this is the worst month for you to do this. Can we please, please revisit this next month? Give me two months."

Kenny inhaled deeply, her eyes narrowing slightly as she processed his request. She could see the stress lines on Camden's face, the weariness that came from juggling work, the upcoming charity event, and now, this intense conversation about their future. But she also knew that this wasn't something she could afford to put off any longer.

"Camden, I understand that you're under a lot of pressure right now, but I'm not asking for something unreasonable. I'm asking for clarity. For a commitment that shows me, we're on the same page about our future. Two more months might seem like a small thing to you, but to me, it feels like more of the same—more waiting, more uncertainty."

Camden reached out and took her hand, his grip firm but gentle. "Kenny, I love you. I don't want to lose you over this. But I'm asking for a little more time because I want to make sure that when we take this step, it's right for both of us. I want to marry you and start a family with you, but I don't want to rush into it because of external pressures."

She met his gaze, searching his eyes for something—anything—that would reassure her. "Camden, this isn't just about Jody's comments or some arbitrary timeline. It's about knowing that we're both committed to the same future. I don't want to keep waiting, wondering if you'll ever be ready. And I can't keep living in this limbo, hoping that one day you'll wake up and decide that I'm the one."

He sighed, rubbing his thumb over the back of her hand. "Kenny, you are the one. I've known that for a long time. But I also know that marriage is a big deal, and I want to make sure we're both absolutely certain before we take that step."

She pulled her hand away, her expression hardening. "I am certain, Camden. I have been certain for a while now. The question is, are you? Because if you're not, then maybe we're not on the same page after all."

Camden's heart sank at the determination in her voice. He knew she was serious—this wasn't just a threat; it was a line in the sand. And he realized that if he didn't make a decision now, he might lose her forever.

"Kenny, I..." He paused, struggling to find the right words.

"I don't want to lose you. But I also don't want to make promises I can't keep. If we're going to do this, I want it to be right. Not rushed, not forced. I'm asking for two months because I need to get everything in order—my work, the charity event, my head. But I promise you, at the end of those two months, I'll be ready. No more delays. No more reassessments."

Kenny studied him for a long moment, weighing his words. Finally, she nodded, though the resolve in her eyes didn't waver. "Two months, Camden. That's all you get. And if you're not ready by then, I'm walking away. Not because I want to, but because I need to protect my future too."

Camden nodded, swallowing the lump in his throat.

The weight of their conversation hung in the air as they finished their meal in relative silence, each lost in their own thoughts. The soothing tones of Anita Baker's "Body and Soul" played in the background.

Camden grimaced at the irony of the words; those could be Kenny's exact sentiments after that heavy conversation. The stakes had just been raised: commit or lose her. He didn't want to lose her; he was going to have to commit body and soul. His single days were numbered, and curiously, he didn't mind that much.

They left the restaurant, hand in hand but with a palpable tension between them. Camden knew that the clock was ticking.

He had two months to prove to Kenny—and to himself— that he was ready for the life they both wanted. And this time, there would be no more extensions.

Chapter Six

The weekend was not as activity-free as he had thought it would be, Camden thought resentfully. He was sitting on the patio, watching Jody on the phone as she effectively and efficiently destroyed his plans to vegetate and do nothing. It was an emergency, she had said; the charity needed its president. There was an issue with two sponsors, the Nelson Construction Company and Deals on Wheels. Both places had not paid their pledged donations, and without that money, the event would be a disaster because they were big donors. And she had insisted on coming over to sort things out together.

Camden sighed, rubbing the bridge of his nose as he listened to Jody's side of the conversation. She was in full crisis mode, her voice calm but with that underlying steel that meant she was determined to fix the problem no matter what.

Why had he agreed to her coming to his place for an urgent

meeting, and why was Kenny finding it so funny?

She pushed her head through the door and grinned at him. She knew he had a date with the couch and his favorite Premier League football match in an hour and that this meeting was grating on his last nerve.

"I am ordering takeout from The Taco Place," Kenny said. "I know what Camden likes. What would you like, Jody?"

"Oh," Jody smiled, "you are such a gracious host, Kenny. I'll have whatever Camden is having."

"You sure about that?" Kenny asked. "Camden likes his tacos extra spicy, with a side of those jalapeño poppers that could make a grown man cry. Most people can't handle the heat."

Jody chuckled, her eyes still glued to her phone screen as she fired off another email. "I'm sure. I could use a little kick today."

Kenny raised an eyebrow, clearly impressed. "Alright, you asked for it. Don't blame me if you're reaching for a glass of milk later."

"Okay," Camden said to Jody, "I'll call Rory Nelson and sort out the Nelson Construction sponsorship. You deal with Deals on Wheels; if you can't get through to Thomas, Kenny will reach him—he is her stepbrother."

"Thomas Sterling is Kenny's stepbrother? Since when?" Jody asked.

"Since five years ago," Camden said. "Kenny's mother married Thomas' father."

"Mmmm," Jody nodded. "That's great."

"And, as you know, Rory Nelson is my best friend." Camden dialed Rory's number while Jody walked to the other end of the patio and dialed Thomas'.

"What's up?" Camden asked when Rory answered.

"Nothing," Rory said. "Want to come over and watch the

match?"

"Okay," Camden said. "I need to get Jody off my back, though. She is at my place, panicking about the sponsorship for the charity event. Apparently, you and Deals on Wheels haven't paid up yet, and she's worried the whole thing might fall apart."

Rory chuckled on the other end of the line. "Ah, that explains why she's blowing up my phone. I've been meaning to get that sorted; I've just been swamped with work. Tell her not to worry; I'll make the payment first thing tomorrow. You are going to participate, aren't you?"

"Yup," Camden said.

"Then I'll show up for the event, too," Rory chuckled. "Make sure you win."

He covered the phone and was talking to someone in the background.

"Jewel said you should take Kenny when you're coming."

"Kenny is washing her hair," Camden said, "and doing her Sunday Reset ritual, and she just ordered tacos."

"Jewel said she is coming over to your place instead," Rory said.

"Fine by me," Camden murmured.

"And bring some of your tacos with you," Rory chuckled. "I love that we live just ten minutes from each other. We have never lived this close before."

"Except in college," Camden said. "I'll be over in a few. I am going to have to hurry Jody out of here. Kenny will kill me if I let Jody intrude on her Sunday Reset."

"Okay, cool," Rory said and hung up.

After hanging up the phone, Jody came over to him. "I got through to Thomas; he said it was an oversight. His manager will sort it out tomorrow."

"Same thing for Rory," Camden got up and stretched. "So,

crisis averted.”

“Why are you getting up?” Jody asked. “I was just about to sit down. I absolutely love the view here. I would live here.”

“It is nice,” Camden said. “But I am going to watch the match with Rory at his place, and Kenny is doing her Sunday Reset. It would be boring hanging out with just her.”

Jody laughed dryly. “I get the hint. I am going. It's truly unfair that you get this view and don’t try to drink it in every minute of every day.”

“Then I wouldn’t get any work done,” Camden said. “Besides, absence makes the heart grow fonder. Whenever I go to work and come back home, it hits me afresh how blessed I am to have this vista.”

“Do you know if all the houses are sold out?” Jody asked.

“I have no clue,” Camden said. “They were priced for snob appeal—just five houses in a super private alcove. I am guessing my neighbors could be anyone. The lots are a good size and quite private.”

“And you all get this fabulous piece of beachfront. I see steps leading down to the sea. Is there a usable beach down there?”

"Yes," Camden nodded. "A rocky outcrop shelters that beach from any prying eyes or casual visitors. It's like having a private slice of paradise. The sand is soft, and the waves are usually gentle. You can swim, sunbathe, or just sit there and listen to the ocean. It's one of the reasons I fell in love with this place."

Jody’s eyes sparkled with interest. “That sounds incredible. I can see why you love it here. I’ve always dreamt of living near the sea, waking up to the sound of the waves every day. It is a dreamy place to live—a perpetual vacation. I wish I could afford a place over here, but I know it is way out of my price point."

"It cost an arm and a leg, but it's worth it," Camden said as he walked her to the patio door. "Sorry about the tacos."

"No problem," Jody said. "I have leftovers in my fridge. I will just mosey on over to my tiny apartment with no remarkable view and eat my lunch all by my lonesome."

Camden looked at her contemplatively. Was he supposed to ask her to stay? He couldn't do that without consulting Kenny, and he knew Kenny would say no. Jody wasn't her friend.

"Babe," he called to Kenny, who was probably in one of the ensuite bathrooms doing her spa day ritual. "Can you come here for a sec?"

Kenny's voice echoed from down the hall. "Give me a minute! Is the taco here already?"

Camden turned back to Jody, who was pretending to examine a seashell on the patio table, though he could tell she was listening keenly to them.

Kenny finally appeared, her hair wrapped in a towel, a face mask still setting on her skin. "What's up?" she asked, her tone light but with an edge that Camden recognized all too well.

"Jody was just about to head out," Camden said, trying to keep things casual. "I am going over to Rory. She mentioned she'd be eating alone, and I thought maybe—"

Kenny shook her head subtly, a look of horror in her eyes. "I'm sure Jody's got plans, don't you, Jody?"

Jody looked up, her smile forced. "Oh, yeah. I've got a ton of things to catch up on."

Camden nodded, feeling caught in the middle. He wanted to be polite and hospitable, but he also wanted Jody gone. "Alright, well, don't be a stranger, Jody. You're welcome here anytime."

Jody's smile softened. She glared at Kenny briefly before returning her gaze to Camden. "Thanks, Camden. I'll see you around."

She turned to leave, and Camden walked her to the door. When the door closed behind Jody, Camden let out a breath he didn't realize he was holding.

Kenny was already back in the hallway, her tone casual but with an underlying firmness. "You didn't need to invite her to stay, you know. I am not particularly fond of her. And don't be fooled by her little excuses to come over here; she warned me she was after you."

"I think she wanted to come and check the place out and was looking for an excuse to see where I lived," Camden replied, heading back to his couch and turning on the television. "I didn't want her to feel as if I was throwing her out just now. Usually, I am a hospitable guy, but today was not the day. I am going to wait on the tacos, and then I am going to bounce."

"Cool," Kenny said.

"By the way, Jewel said she is coming over."

"Now that's a visitor I would love to entertain," Kenny said. "I must tell her to bring her pearly gates nail polish. Love that shade."

****

So, Kenny gave me an ultimatum," Camden said after the match. Their side had lost, and they were morose about it. They needed to talk about something other than their disappointment. They had already critiqued and criticized the match to death.

"What's the ultimatum?" Rory asked, sprawling out on the settee across from him.

"In two months, if I don't give her a response to the marriage question, she's leaving."

"Hmmm," Rory said.

"I need more than an hmmm," Camden threw a pillow at his friend.

"I mean, what's the hold-up?" Rory asked. "You love her; she loves you. You live together. I would think marriage would be a no-brainer by now. You've seen her at her best and worst; you are used to each other's foibles and idiosyncrasies."

"And we have great sex," Camden murmured. "The stuff of dreams."

"And that," Rory said, "that's important! So why aren't you married already?"

"Because what we have is good, perfect. I'm thinking marriage might jinx it," Camden said. "Do you know how many people get married and then break up after being together for a while? The act of marriage jinxes things."

Rory laughed. "Cam, that's just jitters talking. I get it; marriage is a big step. But if you're already living like a married couple and everything's great, what makes you think putting a ring on it will suddenly ruin things?"

Camden shrugged, running a hand through his hair. He needed a haircut. "I don't know, man. It's just... the finality of it, you know? Right now, if things go south, we can just walk away. But marriage? That's a whole different level of commitment. What if it changes things between us?"

Rory shook his head, a grin tugging at the corners of his mouth. "Marriage doesn't change the person you're with. It just makes it official, lets the world know what you already feel. If anything, it should make things stronger."

"But what if it doesn't?" Camden insisted. "What if we get married, and suddenly all these expectations come crashing down on us? What if we start fighting more, or invite other people into our relationship or—"

"Or what if you get married, and it's even better?" Rory countered. "What if marriage is just the next chapter in what you already have, and it's everything you didn't even know you wanted?"

Camden was quiet for a moment, staring at the ceiling. "You make it sound so simple."

Rory laughed again, tossing the pillow back at him. "That's because it is. You're overthinking it. You've got a good thing going with Kenny. Don't let fear mess that up."

Camden caught the pillow and held it to his chest, feeling the weight of Rory's words. "But what if I'm not ready?"

"Then be honest with her," Rory said, his tone more serious now. "But don't string her along. She's given you an ultimatum because she knows what she wants, and she's probably tired of waiting for you to figure it out. If you need more time, tell her that. But don't leave her in limbo."

Camden sighed, knowing his friend was right. "Yeah, you're right. I just... I don't want to lose her."

"Then don't," Rory said simply. "Talk to her. Figure out what's really holding you back. But don't let a good thing slip away because you're scared of what might happen."

Camden nodded. "Thanks, man. I needed that."

"Anytime," Rory said. "You can always talk to my sister about this. You know that. She helped Shay when she was reluctant to get married to Jeremiah and look how that turned out."

"Mercedes?" Camden grimaced. "Nope, not telling my one-time crush that I am afraid of marriage. She'll laugh and wag her finger at me and say, 'Camden, why can't you be serious about anything?'"

Camden imitated Mercedes' voice.

Rory laughed. "It's Dr. Mercedes to you. It's official since last week."

"She went and got her med degree through two pregnancies." Camden whistled. "Superwoman. I am proud of her."

"And she did it all while happily married to Charles," Rory added. "They made it work, and if they can make it work, so can you with Kenny."

"I hear you," Camden nodded.

Chapter Seven

Kenny was packing up to leave work; it was the weekend after a long, hard week. She glanced at her calendar; it had been two weeks since her ultimatum to Camden, and they had six weeks to go until the ultimatum expired. The ultimatum was hanging in the back of her mind like a bad rain cloud. She couldn't help thinking of best-case and worst-case scenarios. The best-case scenario was that Camden proposed, they got married, and they continued on as they had been. The worst case was that she had to move out and back into her apartment, which her younger sister, Kendrea, had been living in since she had left.

The two-bedroom place was hers—her first purchase since she and Jewel had sold an app to Richard Tinsdale, the property developer. So, it wasn't as if leaving Camden meant she would be homeless. Her place wasn't as luxurious as Ridgeview, but it wasn't bad either; it was in a gated community with a decent view of the hills and the sea.

They would split and close their joint account for household expenses, which they contributed to equally every month. Maybe they could split their investment portfolio, too, which had steadily grown for the past two years. Luckily, they didn't have any pets to tussle over. Kenny sighed; why was she being so pessimistic?

Not pessimistic, practical, the voice in her head said. Camden was not going to want to get married. She had no idea why he wasn't pro-marriage. His parents were happily married, and both sets of his grandparents were also married.

His grandparents in Florida had just celebrated sixty-five years together, which was remarkable—not only because of their longevity but also their circumstances. His grandfather was white, from a heavily racist, white supremacist background, and his grandmother was black; she had migrated from Jamaica back in the fifties. They had defied the odds and tied the knot even when it had been forbidden and illegal. In fact, their union had only been recognized after 1967.

Kenny had always admired that about Camden's family—the strength to defy expectations and societal norms. It was the kind of love story that should have inspired Camden to believe in the power of marriage. She couldn't figure it out. He was loyal, committed, and generous in every way that mattered. What was causing the reluctance?

She shoved the last item into her briefcase and fished out her ringing phone from her bag. She was the last person in the office; the rest of her team had left already, so she could talk freely.

"I'm back!" Audra squealed in her ear when Kenny answered her phone.

"Oh my goodness!" Kenny smiled. "Are you serious? You're here in JA, on the rock?"

"Yes, ma'am! I just put down my suitcase in my parents' guest house and had a long shower. I'm ready to breathe in some island air. I have been so cooped up, locked in, and stressed out during my residency. I am ready to party like a rock star! My parents are babysitting Jason, and I'm ready to start looking around for a stepfather for him and a man to hold me down. He has to be at least six feet tall and treat women like they are made of spun glass, not meat.

"I want the whole package—romance, respect, and someone who knows how to make me laugh until I cry. No more settling for less, Kenny. I'm done with the jerks and the wannabes. It's time to find someone who's the real deal.

"So, what's the plan for tonight? I hope you're ready to hit the town with me because I am not wasting a single second of this freedom. We're going to paint this island red!"

Kenny laughed, the excitement in Audra's voice infectious. "Oh, I'm definitely in! But where exactly are we going to find this specimen of manhood for you?"

"My mother said there's a place called Mingles," Audra replied.

"Never heard of it," Kenny said. "But then again, I am more of a house party kind of girl. There's certainly a house party every other weekend in our circle of friends and acquaintances. Somebody is always celebrating something."

"Not interested," Audra snorted. "Your circle is also my circle; I want to meet people I don't know. My mom said Mingles is a classy spot. It can be overrun by people in the medical field and the more sophisticated tourist types, but she and Dad go there when they want to pretend that they are young again."

"Sounds like a geriatric club," Kenny chuckled as she walked out of the office and into the elevator.

"But it's also a place where fellow doctors are," Audra

said. "Remember my plan of marrying a doctor and being a power couple?"

"I remember," Kenny giggled. "I thought all of that was put to rest when you quit med school after getting pregnant by a secret mystery man."

"But I saw the light," Audra said. "I am now back on track."

Kenny laughed. "Jason will be eight this year; can't you give me a hint— even a tiny hint—about who his father is?"

"Nope," Audra chuckled.

"So much for being best friends since kindergarten," Kenny grumbled.

"My mother says something similar when I refuse to tell her too, except there's a hint of motherly blackmail in there, but I am not talking," Audra said, unperturbed. "Anyway, we leave at nine. I'll come and pick you up."

"Nine?" Kenny balked. "That's usually when I am preparing to go to bed!"

Audra laughed. "Not tonight. Tonight we are going to party!"

She hung up, and Kenny glared at the phone. Audra was always bossing her around and telling her what to do since they were three. It seemed as if she was falling back into the regular friendship pattern. She was only going to allow it just this once; after all, her friend had just come back, and there was something comforting about having her oldest friend back in the same vicinity.

****

"Babe, I'll be home late," Camden called almost at the same time she pulled up to the garage. "I am going to my parents' place. Dad had a brilliant idea for our case and graciously wants to share it with me over dinner."

Kenny chuckled. "You sound put out about it."

"This is not how I wanted to spend my Friday night," Camden said. "I had visions of us cuddled up on the sofa, eating our weight in popcorn, and binge-watching that series we've been obsessed with," Camden sighed. "But duty calls, and when Dad gets an idea in his head, there's no stopping him."

"About that," Kenny said, "Audra is here; she wants to go clubbing tonight, and she is coming to pick me up at nine."

"Clubbing?" Camden asked. "Where?"

"Mingles," Kenny said. "Apparently, that's where the doctors hang out, and she is going back to her power couple plan."

Camden laughed out loud. "Mingles? That's Ashton's favorite place on a Friday night. His efforts to find someone from that place have so far been unsuccessful. Tell Audra all the best."

"Maybe there are better pickings with the men than the women," Kenny said.

"It all seems so tedious," Camden said. "Come to think of it, I would probably be visiting Mingles if it were three years ago too. Oh, how the times have changed. I am living a more domesticated life now, and you know what?"

"What?" Kenny asked.

"I like it," Camden said in wonder.

"I like it too," Kenny said. "If it weren't for Audra, I would be hoping for a quiet night too."

"Don't wear anything provocative," Camden said seriously. "I won't be there to appreciate it."

"Okay," Kenny said. "I'll wear pants and a loose top."

"Pants on you are x-rated," Camden murmured. "You have the perfect perky shape. You know what? I am not comfortable with you going to this place without me."

"Your jealousy is duly noted and appreciated," Kenny chuckled, "but I am just going to hang with Audra at this Mingles and be her wingman. That's all, nothing more, nothing less."

"And if someone makes an advance on you?" Camden asked.

"I'll tell them I am in a relationship with a fabulous guy and quickly pass them along to Audra."

"Good girl," Camden said. "I may pull up there after dinner with Dad to keep an eye on you."

"That's so unnecessary," Kenny giggled. "You sound stalkerish."

She entered the house and headed for the shower. "I'll be leaving at nine."

"Okay," Camden said, "see you later."

It took Kenny an hour to get ready. She spun around in the mirror, admiring her handiwork. She had dressed in tight black leather pants and a loose top, which was quite demure at the front but opened at the back. She had finally mastered the glazed makeup look. She looked dewy, glowy, and fresh—just what she was aiming for.

Audra greeted her at the door with astonishment. "Wow, you look awesome!"

"You don't look bad yourself," Kenny said, looking her friend over. Audra was dressed in a little black dress, her long hair down to her waist. She looked tired around the eyes, though; she had lost a lot of weight. Maybe a tad too much.

"I have never known you to lie," Audra said impatiently. "I look tired and thin. I can't have you going out looking better than me; I am the single one! Give me some of what you have."

"What are you talking about?" Kenny asked, looking at her friend in confusion.

"You look gorgeous! Glam me up. Do exactly what you did to yourself to me."

"Oh, that's what you mean," Kenny laughed. "Okay, come on through."

"It's a pity I can't borrow your shape, too," Audra grumbled. "I lost all my curves last year, not that I had much to begin with; residency stressed me out. Do you have an outfit like the one you have on? Mine suddenly looks dated. I thought a little black dress would be sufficient, but I feel frumpy and matronly beside you."

Kenny clapped her hands in glee. "Do you realize how unusual this is? In all of our friendship, I was the less attractive friend—the one everybody overlooked when we went out. The poor one who couldn't pay for herself. The one who got the hand-me-downs and handouts was only tolerated because rich girl Audra insisted I tag along."

"Ah, Kenny," Audra looked at her reprovingly, "you have never been less attractive than me. You were always naturally beautiful and shapely. I envied everything about you when we were younger—your looks, your hair, the fact that you didn't give a hoot about how things looked or how people saw you. You were always so confident, Kenny. I would have traded all the money in the world for that kind of self-assurance back then. You were never 'less' anything— you were just… you."

Kenny blinked, taken aback by Audra's words. "I never knew you felt that way," she admitted softly. "I guess we both had our insecurities."

Audra shrugged, a small smile playing on her lips. "Doesn't everyone? So, what do you say? Help a girl out and make me as fabulous as you are tonight? I am woefully out of the beauty scene; I haven't applied makeup in years. My specialty is lip gloss and some mascara."

Kenny grinned, pulling Audra into a warm hug. "Of course! When I am done with you, the men at Mingles will not know what hit them."

"Deal," Audra agreed, her smile growing as she followed Kenny into the bedroom.

Chapter Eight

It took them twenty minutes to get to Mingles from Ridgeview. It was at the end of the hip strip, a big pink flashing sign covered about half the building, so there was no mistaking that they were in the right place. The parking lot was about half full, which meant they were early.

Kenny glanced at her watch; it was a little after ten. Audra's glam makeover had taken them a while, and then her friend had settled on an outfit from her closet that fit her much better than it had ever fit Kenny. It was a shorts set that Kenny had banished to the back of the closet because of how indecent it had appeared on her. It fit Audra's more modest curves perfectly.

They got out of the car, and the faint sounds of Haddaway's 'What Is Love' could be heard from the parking lot.

"I think this song will still be a banger in the twenty-second century," Audra said, starting to move to the beat.

Kenny grinned. "Yup, played at every school concert back

in the day. Remember those days when we used to sing along and yell, 'Baby, don't hurt me, no more?'"

Audra laughed. "Of course! We didn't even have a baby to hurt us. This is the right song to set the tone for our entrance—let's go inside!"

There was a red carpet entrance and a place to buy their tickets.

"Good evening, beautiful ladies. There are free cocktails upstairs for the ladies from now until twelve," the guy at the ticket desk said. "Upstairs is for conversation and more intimate dancing if you are up for that. Downstairs is straight high energy for the night. We have a special guest DJ who will definitely lift the roof. But if you want a more sedate vibe, then the VIP lounge is far quieter and private if you just want to chat without the hype. You have to pay extra for that."

"Thank you," Audra said, "but I think we are fine for now."

"Sounds well put together," Kenny murmured as they entered the lobby area.

"So where to first?"

"Free cocktails," Audra chuckled. "Non-alcoholic for me, 'cause I am driving."

"Me too," Kenny said. "I have a family event tomorrow. I can't be hungover. I offered to help decorate the place with Kendrea."

She slowed down at the entrance to where the loud, pulsating music was coming from and peeked inside. It had a dark, moody ambiance lit by pulsing neon lights in shades of purple and blue. There was a spacious dance floor as the focal point, surrounded by sleek, minimalistic furniture. The DJ booth was elevated, pumping out loud, bass-heavy beats while the bar was serving colorful cocktails with glowing accents.

The crowd was lively, with people dancing in groups or solo under a glittering disco ball. The DJ was playing Ed Sheeran's 'Shape of You'—the club is not a place to find a lover, so the bar is where I go.

Audra laughed. "I think that's a sign, for us to go to the bar upstairs."

Kenny laughed.

Two guys passed by them, slowed down, and whistled.

"You two here alone?" one of the guys asked.

"Not sure yet," Audra said.

"What do you mean by that?" the shorter of the two asked. "We don't seem good enough for you?"

The guys were mercifully distracted by a scantily clad lady who passed them before Audra could answer, and they escaped upstairs, laughing together.

"He was so aggressive," Audra said. "I'm actually not mad at it."

Upstairs, the atmosphere shifted dramatically. The lighting was softer, with warm hues and dimmed overhead lamps, creating a more intimate setting. Comfortable lounge chairs and plush velvet couches filled the space, offering a place to relax and chat. There was a small dance floor with a more mellow vibe, where couples swayed to the softer beats of an R&B track. The music was much lower, allowing for conversation without shouting.

Audra exhaled in relief. "Now, this is more my speed."

Kenny nodded, glancing around. "Yeah, definitely a nice change. I can actually hear myself think up here."

They made their way to the bar, where the bartender greeted them with a smile. "What can I get you?"

"Something non-alcoholic for me," Audra said. "Surprise me."

Kenny leaned against the bar. "Same here. We're staying responsible tonight."

As they waited for their drinks, Kenny scanned the room. It was a calmer, more sophisticated crowd up here—people lounging, chatting, and enjoying their drinks. She noticed a few familiar faces, but none she felt compelled to approach.

"Much better crowd," Kenny remarked. "And no aggressive guys. Maybe your doctor fellow is up here."

Audra laughed. "From your mouth to God's ears."

The bartender returned with their drinks—two tall glasses filled with vibrant, fruity mocktails.

They clinked glasses and settled into the plush chairs by the window, where the lights across the sea twinkled beyond the glass.

Audra instantly started looking around, her eyes scanning the patrons.

"Why am I seeing familiar faces?" Audra groaned. "My parents' friends. Is that Uncle Peter?"

Kenny followed her gaze to a few people leaning against the bar, dressed to the nines, chatting like they owned the place.

"It's a small town. Downstairs is where the younger people are."

Audra swiveled around and then made a gasping, choking sound.

"You okay?" Kenny asked.

"I, er…" Audra had trouble speaking. She turned back to Kenny, real fear on her face. "I don't think I like it up here anymore."

"Why?" Kenny frowned. "Who did you see?"

"I, ah…" Audra swallowed. "Someone I knew from a long, long time ago."

"Who?" Kenny was looking over her shoulder.

"Don't look!" Audra hissed. "I don't want him to see me."

"Okay," Kenny said, subsiding in her chair. "At least give me a hint about who it is."

Audra sipped her drink and carefully placed it on the table in front of them. "Kenny, I don't think I can stay here," she whispered, her voice tight.

Kenny furrowed her brow and leaned in closer. "Audra, seriously, who did you see? What's going on?"

Audra glanced around quickly as if someone might overhear them. "It's… it's my, er, neighbor—my parents' neighbor from years ago."

Kenny's eyes widened. "So?"

"He, er…" Audra inhaled. "I had a crush on the guy. I never told you about it."

"Okay," Kenny nodded. "So we avoid him. Just keep an eye out for him; he won't ruin your night."

Audra relaxed a fraction but still looked uneasy.

Kenny strained her neck, looking around and trying to figure out who could have made Audra this uncomfortable.

And then a male voice said, "Fancy meeting you here, ladies." Kenny looked around; it was Ashton Byfield, Camden's cousin.

"Oh hey, Ashton," Kenny smiled.

"Hey, Ashton," Audra said. "What's going on?"

"Nothing much." Ashton pulled up a chair. "I heard you were away, Audra."

"I was. Now I'm back," Audra said. "I thought you were away too."

"I was," Ashton grinned. "Now I'm back working at the family firm, tussling with my younger cousin and brother for a partnership position. I'm also single and looking. How about you?"

"Same," Audra said. "Working at the family practice,

except I have no competition. I'm single and looking, but I'm not interested in a lawyer, sorry."

"Ouch," Ashton said.

"It's not you, it's me," Audra replied. "I have particular requirements."

"I see," Ashton sighed. "You know, Mingles is the only place I've come to socialize, and I've gotten overlooked because I'm a lawyer. It has happened to me twice now, and both times it crushed my spirits a little."

Kenny chuckled. He didn't seem crushed at all.

He turned to her. "Kenny, what's wrong with me?"

"Nothing," Kenny said, smiling. "Maybe it's the place. Maybe you should try another spot. Physically, I can see nothing wrong with you."

"It's true," Ashton said. "I have been blessed with the Byfield good looks."

"It's definitely not your looks," Kenny agreed. "You look a lot like my boyfriend, and he is gorgeous."

"I'm five years older," Ashton chuckled. "So it's the other way around; he looks a lot like me."

Kenny nodded. They had the same shaped head, nose, and high forehead. He was quite handsome.

"Camden told me that this is your favorite spot these days," Kenny said, grinning.

Ashton laughed. "Only on a Friday night. I have no time otherwise. I'm sure Camden told you that we are under pressure at the office to perform like hamsters on a wheel for promotion to junior partner and that he is my competition."

"He did tell me," Kenny nodded. "You know I'm rooting for him, don't you?"

"As you should," Ashton nodded. "Where is he, by the way?" he asked, looking around.

"At his father's for dinner," Kenny said. "I just came with

Audra here to hang out for a while. Maybe we can get in a dance or two."

Ashton nodded. "This is a good spot for dancing. I prefer the older type music up here. Want to dance?"

"Nobody else is dancing," Kenny said, looking around at the dance floor.

"There's one person," Ashton said, pointing to a woman in a short red dress who was putting on a performance. She was alone on the dance floor, swinging her hips to Alicia Keys' "Girl on Fire." She was putting on quite a show.

"We can't intrude," Kenny giggled. The woman was jerking her body like she was being electrocuted, and a group of men at a table in the half-dark were cheering her on.

Even Audra turned around and watched her. "She is the definition of dancing like no one is watching. Now that's confidence."

"I would never be so bold," Kenny chuckled, then paused. "That's Jody!"

"Jody Levy," Audra whistled. "I didn't know she was so flexible."

"How do you guys know her?" Ashton asked.

"We went to the same college. Audra did some classes with her, but I didn't," Kenny said. "She is a physiotherapist. She treated Camden for an injury five years ago and introduced him to the Cycle Club. She is the current vice president."

"Intriguing," Ashton said. "Camden's cycle club? And he didn't say a word about this girl. Is she single?"

"As far as I know," Kenny answered quickly. "She is always sniffing around Camden. I'd be surprised if she had a man and was so thirsty over mine."

But Ashton was too late. One of the guys from the table who was cheering her dancing went over to her and whispered in her ear. She started having a giggle fest with him.

"Bummer," Ashton murmured. "Lucked out again. Tonight is not my night."

"Don't just give up," Kenny urged him. "Go over."

"Not in the mood for a competition," Ashton said, and then his eyes lit up. "Isn't that Jairo Jones?"

He waved toward a tall and muscular man dressed in black who was heading down the stairs back into the main lounge with a group of friends. The man looked handsome and dangerous at the same time.

Audra audibly groaned and swiveled around to hide her face.

Ashton was waving like a maniac. Jairo looked over and started toward them.

Kenny was confused. "Who is Jairo Jones?" she asked aloud.

"You're kidding, aren't you?" Ashton replied. "He recently retired from the Premier League; he was the leading scorer for Arsenal, one of the best strikers the league has seen in the past decade. His retirement was all over the news!" Ashton exclaimed, clearly starstruck as he waved Jairo over. "Of course, I went to school with him out here in Jamaica. I knew him before he was famous."

"Jairo Jones... the name sounds so familiar. Oh, snap," Kenny whispered, suddenly realizing why Audra was acting so strange. "Jairo Jones was your neighbor! You remember we used to make fun of his family? They won the lottery and moved into your neighborhood. His mother was a perfect candidate for Keeping Up Appearances, Jamaican Edition. Wait a minute. If her son is so successful now, she must be insufferable these days."

Audra groaned again, keeping her face hidden. "Please

don't let him come over here, Kenny. Please."

Kenny was now more curious than ever. "Wait, what's going on? Why are you hiding from him? Is he the person you saw earlier?"

"Yes," Audra sighed, glancing over at Ashton, who was still eagerly waving Jairo over like an old friend. "We... had a thing a couple of years ago."

Kenny's eyes widened in realization. "He's Jason's father, isn't he?"

Audra groaned. "I'm pleading the fifth."

"We are in Jamaica; there is no fifth, and this is not a court of law." Kenny chuckled. "As I live and breathe, I've finally found out who your baby daddy is."

"Shut up and stop it," Audra said fiercely.

Before Kenny could retort, Jairo Jones reached their table. He was even more imposing up close; his jaw was the definition of chiseled. His eyes were an unusual shade of brown, almost like a paper bag. Maybe it was a tan color, or was it hazel? The same shade as Audra's son, Jason. And the plot thickened.

"Ashton! Good to see you, man." Jairo bumped fists with Ashton. "How long has it been?"

"Nine years," Ashton said. "I last saw you when you came out here for your bachelor party."

Jairo nodded. "Oh yeah. Good times."

He looked at Kenny and smiled. "Good evening, pretty lady."

"Good evening," Kenny smiled back. "My name is Kenny Carter."

He nodded and then looked over at Audra. His smile faltered, turning into something more complicated. "Audra Beckles," he said, his voice softer.

Audra forced a tight smile, her face betraying the tension

she was feeling. "Jairo."

Kenny glanced between them, sensing the thick tension in the air. "Well, this just got interesting," she muttered under her breath.

"Can we talk?" Jairo asked Audra. He hooked his thumb toward the corner of the area where he had just come from with his friends.

Audra inhaled raggedly and got up. "Of course, sure."

She looked back at Kenny. "Soon be back."

Kenny nodded.

"Don't worry, I'll keep you company," Ashton said beside her. "I should have known she would go off with Jairo."

"Why?" Kenny asked. "He is not a doctor."

"That doesn't matter where women are concerned; they claim they have a type, and then a professional athlete comes their way, and that's it, poof, the type is out of the window."

Kenny chuckled. "I don't know, Audra is insistent on her life plan. Her one consistent plan through the years, ever since we were children, was that she would marry a doctor, and the two of them would be a power couple like her parents. You said you last saw him at a bachelor's party. Is he married?" Kenny asked.

"Not sure," Ashton shrugged. "People get married and divorced so fast these days; who knows? Enough about Jairo. I've always wanted to ask why they call you Kenny? What is it short for?"

"Nothing," Kenny said. "I am just plain old Kenny."

"So, there's Jenny and Penny or Tenny," Ashton mused, "all feminine-sounding names, and your parents named you Kenny? When Camden said he was living with Kenny, I almost fell out of my chair; I know Jamaicans are not so liberal with same-sex relationships, and yet there he was waxing poetic about you."

Kenny chuckled. "My father's name was Kenneth, and he named all five of us, beginning with Ken. The oldest is Kenneth Junior, his only son."

Ashton nodded. "Makes sense."

"Then there were four girls. I'm the oldest, so I was named plain old Kenny. The sister following me is Kenisha, the other sister is Kenice, and my baby sister is Kendrea."

"So, where are your sisters? Any of them single?" Ashton asked.

"No, sorry," Kenny laughed. "Kenisha and Kenice are married. Kendrea has a boyfriend. Ashton, with your looks and background finding somebody shouldn't be that hard. Why do you sound so desperate?"

"Tell me, Kenny, where am I supposed to find a female companion who is beautiful and kind, can put up with my working hours, and does not feel abandoned? Someone who is independent enough to pursue her own interests but still wants to spend time with me? It feels like looking for a needle in a haystack these days."

Kenny tilted her head, giving him a curious look. "You really think it's that hard?"

"Harder than you'd imagine," Ashton sighed. "I've met women who are beautiful, and I've met women who are kind, but finding someone who's both? Add in the fact that my work is so time-consuming... it's like they lose interest fast."

Kenny shrugged. "Maybe you're looking in the wrong places. Or maybe you're putting too much pressure on it."

Ashton looked at her thoughtfully. "And where would you suggest I look, Ms. Kenny? I can't really clone you, can I? And all your sisters are taken."

Kenny smiled, shaking her head. "Sometimes the best things show up when you stop looking so hard. Let life happen a bit. You might be surprised at who crosses your path when you least expect it. Maybe she was always there, and you just overlooked her."

He laughed. "Is that what happened with you and Camden?"

"Something like that," Kenny said. "We just hung out together, and then we realized we didn't want to hang out with anyone else. We've known each other for years, since prep school."

Ashton nodded. "I should go and look through my prep school albums and see who I'm overlooking."

Kenny laughed.

They spoke for a while. Kenny realized in astonishment that Ashton was really fun to be around. When their paths had crossed in the past, it was usually at family functions and only fleetingly. He had the predominant Byfield male trait: he could put a person at ease in no time. She enjoyed their conversation; he was knowledgeable about many things.

"Why did you come back to Jamaica?" Kenny asked after they discussed his surfing experiences in California.

"I got homesick," Ashton said. "My dad kept harping on and on about legacy and the family business and how my younger brother and cousin were taking the family business and brand seriously, while I didn't care. So, that coupled with the obscene house prices in Cali, a failed relationship that I thought would have gone somewhere but didn't, and a run-in with one of the partners at the law firm where I was slaving away like the lowly associate I was, I decided I could do better. I thought I would be welcomed with a red carpet rollout and handed the golden keys of partnership, but instead, I had to prove myself. Not only that, but I also had to battle for the position over my younger brother and cousin, who have far less experience than I do. It's demeaning, I tell you."

"Camden said you would all make partners eventually," Kenny said. "I don't see why there has to be a battle."

"The first person who makes junior partner will more than likely get the nod to be senior partner when the time comes," Ashton said. "Besides, this little battle is not purely for entertainment; it's to see who wants it the most, who has the best legal mind of the three of us, who can think on their feet the fastest, and who can ultimately lead the firm."

Kenny nodded. "I think Camden would do a great job."

Ashton laughed. "Of course, you would think so. I sort of think so too, but I would need way more liquor to admit that out loud."

Just then, Audra came over with Jairo in tow.

"Say, Kenny, can you hitch a ride home with Ashton? Jairo and I are going to bounce."

"Just like that?" Kenny looked between the two of them.

"We need to talk somewhere much quieter," Audra whispered in her ear. "I'll call you tomorrow."

"Okay," Kenny nodded.

She looked over at Ashton when they left. "Audra is gone; I might as well go home."

Ashton nodded. "The night is still young. Stay a while; keep me company. It's nice talking to someone without the added pressure of romance."

Kenny sighed. "Okay, but I need to go home by twelve."

Chapter Nine

Ashton made her laugh for the entire journey home. Kenny was still laughing when she let herself into the house. She heard the television going upstairs in the family room and realized that Camden was fast asleep in front of it.

"Cam," Kenny whispered.

"Huh?" Camden looked at her, bleary-eyed. "Kenny, where've you been? I called you like a hundred times."

"I never heard the phone," Kenny said. "The club was so loud."

"I am going to bed," Camden said. "Talk to you tomorrow."

Kenny nodded; it was a quarter to one, but she was too keyed up to sleep. She went and had a shower, smiling to herself when she thought about Ashton. He was good company; she would lean on Camden to invite him over.

As soon as her head hit the pillow, she was out like a light but was rudely awakened by Camden sitting beside her, a cup of tea in his hand, speaking on her phone.

"Do you have to have a telephone conversation over my head?" Kenny groaned, turning her back to him. "What time is it?"

"Ten o'clock," Camden said.

"I have to get up and help Kendrea with the decorations for the party."

"She's the one I'm talking to," Camden said. "She wants to know if you got the gift on behalf of your mother's side of the family."

"Yes," Kenny pulled the pillow over her head. "I did, just as discussed."

"Is it made of wood?"

"Yes, wood for the fifth anniversary," Kenny murmured. "And yes, I had all of our names etched into the craft. It's a model boat bought from the recommended vendor in the craft market. I told the guy to etch the Carter Sterling family on the side. It's gorgeous."

Camden faithfully reported to her sister, who she could clearly hear saying, "And tell her to get up; she has obligations."

Camden chuckled and then hung up.

And then Kenny didn't hear anything more. She closed her eyes, trying to recapture the peace she had a few moments ago while she was in dreamless slumber. Camden pulled the pillow from her head.

"Who the hell is AB?"

"Alexander Bell, inventor of the telephone," Kenny said sleepily, pulling the pillow back over her head.

"Kenny," Camden said seriously. "There is a message on your phone from AB, saying he had fun with you last night and that you should do it again sometime. And he wants to know if you have gotten up yet."

"Tell him no," Kenny murmured.

"Who is AB?" Camden asked again, irritated.

"Your cousin, Ashton Byfield. We hung out last night after Audra ditched me for Jairo Jones, and then he dropped me home. Why didn't you tell me he was so much fun?"

"You hung out with my cousin?" Camden asked. "He is my competition!"

"Uh-huh," Kenny murmured.

"Traitor." Camden stood up. "I hope he didn't make a move on you."

"No, he didn't," Kenny chuckled. "He put the moves on Audra, but she shut him down and told him he wasn't a doctor."

Camden laughed.

"If you are not out of bed in five minutes, I am going to wet you up," Camden said.

"No!" Kenny sat up in bed and then groaned, propping herself on the headboard. "Have some pity on me, Camden Byfield. I am no longer used to going to bed late. I am too old for this lifestyle."

"I agree," Camden nodded. "You shouldn't go clubbing; you should have been in bed by nine, all nicely tucked in and waiting for me, not chatting it up with my cousin."

"He is a nice guy," Kenny said. "We had a great conversation."

"He is trying to steal you from me." Camden punched Ashton's number from her phone. "I am going to have to nip this in the bud before the guy catches feelings."

"Oh, whatever," Kenny stumbled out of bed.

She could hear Camden warning Ashton not to be friendly with his girl. She didn't hear Ashton's response, but she knew they went off talking about something else on her phone, which probably needed charging.

"Charge my phone when you're done!" she yelled out.

"Okay," was Camden's muffled response.

****

The Sunday anniversary dinner at her mother and stepfather's place was going to be packed with all of their children and children's spouses. Her mother had married Ralph Sterling five years ago after they met at a school principals' convention. She was a widow with five children, and he was a widower with four. They both had not expected to find love again, but here they were with nine children between them. They were both in their mid-fifties.

Their attempts to blend the Carter and Sterling families have been effortless so far. They had regular family gatherings at their newly acquired four-bedroom homestead, where they enjoyed farming their two acres and throwing family parties by the poolside.

Her sister, Kendrea, knocked on her window as soon as she drove up.

Kenny wound down the window. "You took your time getting here. I had to rope Thomas into helping me with the décor."

"So I'm not needed then?" Kenny said drolly. "I can go and take a nap?"

"No, you can't," Kendrea snorted. "Thomas just hung one piece of decoration and is panting like he ran a mile."

Kenny laughed and got out of the car. "Where are Mom and Ralph?"

"In their suite," Kendrea said. "Probably doing gag-worthy stuff; it is their anniversary, after all."

"Bleh," Kenny made a face.

Kendrea nodded. "Exactly. Now tell me what has you so groggy this morning."

"Went out with Audra last night." Kenny entered the poolside area. Thomas was lying like a beached whale in one of the lounge chairs. He was huge, the fattest she had ever seen him.

"He has gotten bigger," Kenny whispered to Kendrea. "I haven't seen him in like six months. What has he been doing?"

"I have no clue," Kendrea shrugged. "Maybe eating and playing the stock market. He is the opposite of everything they tell you to do to be successful. I don't understand how he does it. I don't understand him."

"How come you don't understand him?" Kenny chuckled. "Isn't he your boyfriend?"

"Stop that foolishness," Kendrea muttered. "I went out with him for one date so he could save face at the Chamber of Commerce dinner last year. He is my stepbrother—nothing more, nothing less."

"But he is so cute," Kenny said. "If Thomas decides to lose that fat, he is going to be a stunner. You should get in there while you can. All the pretty girls like you who shun him now will be hunting him down like a rare gem."

Kendrea rolled her eyes. "No thanks."

Thomas cracked an eye open, obviously having listened to their conversation. "Hey, Kenny. Quite disappointed to hear you say that, Kendrea. We kissed, and you liked it."

"Liar!" Kendrea protested. "And why were you eavesdropping?"

"Ah, I knew you two were serious," Kenny chuckled.

"I am not going to argue and let you two rile me up," Kendrea huffed. "Grab that box, Kenny. It has wooden letters that reads 'Happy Anniversary.' We'll use this string."

They worked together while Thomas chit-chatted.

"Say, Kenny," he said after hauling himself out of the

lounge chair and helping her hold one end of the string as she slotted in the letters. "I bought one of the Ridgeview houses. How is it living there?"

"You bought one?" Kenny widened her eyes. "That's a whole lot of money."

"Yep," Thomas nodded. "I intended to use it as a fancy Airbnb, but I quite like the idea of living somewhere nice. Maybe I can coerce your sister to move in with me."

"It's never going to happen," Kendrea said waspishly. "It's marriage or nothing, bud. No offense, Kenny."

"None taken," Kenny said. "I used to say that too. Now look at me—a live-in girlfriend with no ring in sight."

"Then will you marry me, Kendrea?" Thomas asked. "We did have that one kiss."

"Lose the weight first," Kendrea said snarkily. "Then ask me properly. You had better hope I am not with someone else by then."

Thomas nodded. "Okay."

Kenny laughed.

The event went smoothly; all the children except her brother, who was in Canada, showed up to celebrate with Grace and Ralph Sterling. Camden sat beside her, his hand draped over her chair. They were being entertained by the same cabaret singer—a friend of one of her step-siblings—who had serenaded the couple at their wedding.

He was belting out the song 'Stay With You' by John Legend. Kenny was rocking to the tune and sang along to the chorus. She glanced at Camden; he was looking introspective while nodding his head to the song. What was he thinking, she wondered? It was a classic ride-or-die song, a classic commitment song. Was he reflecting on their situation? The ultimatum she had given him? They had six weeks left. Would this be his sentiment?

Her gaze lingered on him, searching his face for any sign of what might be going through his mind. Time was ticking away, and each passing day brought them closer to the moment of truth. Would he choose for them to stay together in a formalized situation, or would he opt out?

"We've been together for a while now, we're growing stronger every day now. It feels so good, and there is no doubt I will stay with you," John Legend crooned, the words wrapping themselves around her like a warm embrace. Their relationship had never been so tested, and yet here they were, standing at the edge of something new and terrifying. Six weeks left to decide whether they were meant to be in it for the long haul or if they would walk away from what they had built. The thought made her stomach knot.

Camden turned slightly, meeting her eyes. His introspective expression softened, a small smile playing on his lips, but the weight of everything unsaid hung between them. Was this his way of telling her he was all in, or was he just enjoying the song, having no deep thoughts about it?

She returned his smile, though her heart was heavy with uncertainty. If this song reflected any sentiment he had toward her, she'd know soon enough. Six weeks wasn't long, and yet it felt like a lifetime. Would he stay with her—through the ups and downs, through everything life threw at them? Or would the clock run out and, with it, their time together?

After the event, Kenny was busy securing lunch for herself and Camden from the leftovers when she caught him and her mother in a deep conversation, which they cut off when they saw her coming.

"It was a lovely party as usual, Mom," Kenny said, kissing her mother's cheek.

"And it's all thanks to you children. I am blessed to

have such fabulous children and stepchildren," Grace said, hugging her tightly. "We should have lunch next week. And Camden," she turned to him, "we should get together too. Don't get too busy for me."

Camden hugged her. "I'll try to carve out some time, but not next weekend; the cycling club has a charity event."

Grace nodded. "I know. I hope you win; be careful."

"Yes, Mom," Camden nodded.

He took the containers from Kenny, and they exited together as they called out goodbyes to the rest of the family.

"So what were you and my mom talking about so intently?" Kenny asked.

"She was asking me why I was waiting to marry you." Camden looked at her and grinned. "The usual interrogation—nothing new."

"And what did you tell her?" Kenny asked, intrigued.

"I told her that I was afraid of marriage because of a traumatic event in my life, but I am working on overcoming my fears and that you gave me an ultimatum with which I am working. She seemed satisfied with that answer."

"What traumatic event did you have that made you afraid of marriage?" Kenny asked, confused.

"I'll tell you at another time," Camden said, kissing her on the cheek. "See you at home."

Kenny was confused. "I thought we told each other everything. I know everything about you, remember?"

"A man has his secrets," Camden laughed as he got into his car. "Can we continue this conversation at home, preferably with rosemary tea? I think I overate; I need something to settle my stomach."

Kenny nodded. "Okay. I'll make it when I get there."

****

They were cuddling on the sofa with the lights off. The smell of rosemary mint tea still lingered in the air. They opened the patio doors and silently looked at the pattern of the outside lights as they bounced off the walls. Camden had his head on Kenny's belly.

"Is your stomach settled now?" Kenny asked.

"Yep," Camden murmured. "Somewhat. It's getting there."

"So, are you ready to tell me about the traumatic event that caused you to be afraid of marriage?"

"Not really," Camden said. "I've never told anyone but my therapist. But it was so long ago now, I don't even remember her advice."

"But you remember the trauma, and it has affected your views on marriage."

"Yup," Camden murmured.

"What could it be?" Kenny mused. "How old were you?"

"Ten," Camden said.

"What could be traumatic for a ten-year-old?" Kenny pondered. "Your parents aren't divorced. You never had to deal with a revolving door of partners in either of your parents' lives."

Camden snorted.

"What?" Kenny asked. "That's it? Did your mom or your dad cheat? You found out, and it left you traumatized?"

Camden sighed. "Not exactly. It's more nuanced than that. But I was sufficiently grossed out by it that I sort of blocked it out of my mind. But the feeling stayed, you know?"

Kenny ran her fingers through Camden's short curls, waiting patiently for him to speak. "So, what happened?"

Camden shifted uncomfortably, pulling his knees a little closer to his chest. "I walked in on something I shouldn't have seen," he started slowly. "I really am not up to talking about it right now."

Kenny chuckled. "Why? Delicate Camden ate too much and can hardly speak?"

Camden tickled her belly. "Take that back."

"No!" Kenny squealed. "Are you going to tell me or not?"

"Maybe," Camden said, "but not now. Now I want to kiss you all over."

"I thought you were recovering," Kenny said breathlessly. "And incapable of doing anything strenuous, including talking."

"I am miraculously cured," Camden murmured, kissing her all the way up to her lips. "I love you," he said before taking her mouth in a devouring kiss.

"I love you too," Kenny gasped.

Chapter Ten

"So this is the last meeting before the Cycle Club's big event," Jody announced on Thursday evening at Howie's Pub.

Kenny was there only because Camden's car was being serviced, and he needed a lift. She vaguely heard the speeches from her position at the back of the room. She wasn't actively listening because she had a ton of work to complete, and it would extend into the weekend.

She tuned in when Camden got up to speak.

"I am happy that our club is not just a place for enjoyment and exercise but that we can look outward."

Camden's voice carried easily across the small pub, commanding the attention of even those who, like Kenny, had been only half-listening.

"Our rides and our camaraderie are important, of course," Camden continued, "but what's even more vital is the impact we're making on the community. With our fundraising efforts and outreach programs, we're not just cycling for ourselves. We're cycling for the people who need us."

A smattering of applause followed though Kenny noticed Camden's eyes weren't on the audience. They flicked briefly to the back, where she sat. She smiled at him proudly and gave him a thumbs-up.

She looked back at her screen. Several messages had come up from her team, and one from Ashton Byfield.

She opened his message. It contained a picture of him in a clown hat with a red nose, which was obviously AI-generated.

Kenny chuckled.

"I just messed up big time with some documents, and I desperately need to reach Camden. He is not answering his phone. He said you would pick him up, so I am assuming he is with you. Can you please let him know I clowned around and found out? He'll know what I am talking about."

Kenny was in the middle of replying when Jody came up behind her.

"Oh my gosh, that's him," Jody said, pointing to the clown picture on the screen.

"Huh?" Kenny looked behind her and then lowered her computer screen. "Don't you know it's impolite to creep up behind people?"

"This is a public place," Jody hissed. "And you have no right to tell me about politeness or otherwise. That's the guy I saw you cheating on Camden with at Mingles. I have been debating telling Camden, but I held back. Not anymore, Missy. You should be ashamed of yourself. Camden is a good man."

Kenny frowned. "You are jumping to conclusions."

"I am not," Jody said stubbornly. "I saw you with my own eyes. I even took a couple of pictures. Showing you talking and laughing with this guy and leaning close. At first, I thought you were with Camden. You seemed so relaxed and happy, but then I saw you get into his car in the parking lot and realized it wasn't Camden's car. The guy resembles Camden, though. You obviously have a type. Oh, you are one shameless girl."

Kenny inhaled, seriously debating whether she should defend herself to Jody, then shrugged it off. Let her think what she wanted.

"You are despicable," Jody was passionately saying, "a cheater, a disgrace. Someone needs to protect Camden from you."

"Don't you have anything better to do?" Kenny sneered.

"You don't deserve him," Jody shot back.

"But I guess you do?" Kenny raised her eyebrows.

"I do," Jody nodded. "And when I get him, I will never cheat. In fact, we'd be married in mere months. I am going to tell Camden about you."

"Go ahead," Kenny said snidely. "Tell him I'm having an affair with his cousin Ashton and see if he doesn't laugh you out of the room."

Jody blinked in surprise, momentarily thrown off balance. "Cousin?" she muttered under her breath, then regained her composure. "Somehow, I had you pegged as a woman with moral character. I guess I was wrong."

Jody glared at her and walked away.

Kenny rolled her eyes and waved to Camden when he caught her gaze from across the room.

He came over. "What were you arguing with Jody about?" he whispered. "I could see the two of you hissing like cats squaring off in a fight."

"She's crazy," Kenny smirked. "Never mind. I'm not going to let Jody affect my peace. Ashton is trying to reach you—said he got himself into clownery."

"Oh dang," Camden muttered, getting up. "I asked him to do one thing. And to do it my way. I'm going to strangle him. I have to go back to the office urgently."

Kenny nodded. "Okay, I guess I'll just work there. It's far quieter and Jody-free."

They were almost out the door when Jody stopped them. "Camden, leaving so soon?" She looked between Camden and Kenny with a forced smile.

"Unfortunately," Camden said, "something came up. I'm going to the office to strangle Ashton."

"Oh my," Jody gasped, dramatically putting her hand over her heart. "So Kenny confessed."

"What?" Camden frowned.

"Violence is never the answer," Jody said. "You should be angry at her, not at him."

Kenny chuckled.

Jody glared at her. "Did Kenny tell you what really happened, not a watered down version?"

"She did," Camden nodded. "I'm sorry, but I'll have to miss the mixer this evening. See you Sunday morning."

Jody's face fell, her disappointment clear. "Oh… Sunday. Right."

"Yep," Camden smiled warmly before turning away with Kenny throwing his arms over her shoulder.

They left Jody standing there, obviously puzzled at their chumminess.

****

The Byfield and Byfield law offices were quiet at six in the evening. The receptionist's desk was empty, but it was obvious that office hours had not ended. She could hear the low buzzing of muted conversations and the ringing of telephones. It was to be expected for a multipurpose law firm.

Camden often described the three-story building as the place that didn't sleep. Kenny looked at the directory for the core specialties: corporate law, real estate law, family law, estate planning/probate, personal injury, and criminal defense.

"You can use my office, Kenny," Camden said. "I am going up to the third floor to see what Ashton did to my briefing."

"Where is your office again?" Kenny asked. "I haven't gotten the official tour yet since you guys relocated, remember? You promised me one at the Christmas party, but we didn't get around to touring. You dragged me home and had your wicked way with me because you said you couldn't wait."

Camden chuckled. "Oh yeah, that's right. Would you be terribly offended if I asked you to look at the directory and take the tour yourself?"

"No, I'm good," Kenny replied, looking around the spacious first floor. "I'll manage just fine."

Camden kissed her quickly and then entered the elevator.

When Camden disappeared behind the elevator doors, Kenny lingered a moment, taking in the feel of the office around her. Despite the muted sounds of phones and voices in the background, the place had an air of tranquility.

She glanced at the directory again, mentally tracing the building's layout. Camden had often raved about the firm's efficient design, with each department seamlessly connected yet distinctly separate.

The first floor was occupied by the client-facing departments—family law, personal injury, and estate planning. It was designed to be welcoming but professional, with comfortable waiting areas and large meeting rooms where clients could speak privately with their attorneys. The walls here were a soothing shade of cream, accented by dark wood trim and soft lighting that made the whole space feel warm, almost inviting.

Kenny wandered past the family law section, her curiosity piqued by the tasteful decor. Camden's mother really had outdone herself; Lorraine Byfield's interior design firm was responsible for the decor.

The space felt intimate without being intrusive. She glanced at one of the meeting rooms where an older couple sat, speaking with an attorney who appeared to be explaining some documents.

Kenny continued down the hall, noticing the shift in ambiance as she passed into the personal injury section. The decor was slightly different here—stronger colors, which she figured symbolized action.

Camden's office was on the second floor; he specialized in real estate law. She took the stairs instead of the elevator and headed for his office. The second floor was just as professionally done. The walls were adorned with tasteful art—none of it ostentatious, just enough to give the space character.

Camden's office was just as she imagined—a large, modern space with sleek furnishings and a minimalist style that still managed to feel comfortable. The desk was neatly organized, but a hint of Camden's personal life peeked through in the form of a framed photo of them from a vacation last summer. Kenny smiled as she walked around the room, running her hand along the edge of the desk.

She sat down in one of the guest chairs, pulled out her laptop, and let the quiet envelop her. It was back to work for her. She had an idea of what the third floor looked like; it had a vast conference room with an unfettered view of the sea and the senior partners' offices. That was where the firm had its annual Christmas party last year.

As Kenny settled into the chair, she let her fingers hover over the keys of her laptop for a moment, allowing the memories of last year's Christmas party to wash over her. The third floor had been beautifully decorated, with twinkling lights and festive garlands lining the large windows that framed the panoramic view of the sea. Camden had pulled her aside during the party, away from the crowd, and they'd stood together, gazing out at the water. It had been one of those rare moments of quiet amid the holiday chaos, and she'd felt closer to him than ever.

Now, sitting in his office, she smiled at the thought. This place—this firm—had become an important part of Camden's life. She remembered how nonchalant he had been about the family business when they were growing up, but now he was dedicated to it.

Kenny glanced at the framed photo on his desk again, a little memento of their time together. It was taken on their grueling cross-country cycling trip; they had taken on the challenge to cycle to Kingston and back. The picture was captured when they returned; the two were smiling, a little sunburned, but happy.

She knew Camden kept his private life closely guarded at work, but seeing that photo felt like an unspoken acknowledgment of her importance in his life.

With a sigh, she turned her attention back to her laptop. There was work to be done, and she needed to make the most of the quiet while Camden dealt with Ashton and his briefing upstairs. She clicked open a document and began typing, the soft clacking of the keys filling the silence.

And then Audra called.

"Thought you had forgotten me," Kenny said. "You left me out to dry Friday night with Ashton."

"I know, I'm sorry," Audra said. "Seeing Jairo again hit me for six; I didn't want to talk about it."

"What's the big secret with him being your baby daddy? Why hide that?" Kenny chuckled. "Is he married?"

"He's divorced," Audra said. "It's a long story."

"Okay," Kenny replied, glancing at her computer. "I have time."

"I can't tell you now," Audra whispered. "I have a ton of things to do. Do you know how much work is involved in relocating with an uncooperative eight-year-old? He's right here beside me, throwing an everlasting tantrum about his toys that somehow didn't make it in our packing boxes."

"I quieted him down with ice cream. Yes, I am that mother. Sometimes, we just need a sliver of peace and quiet, and if ice cream is the answer, so be it."

Kenny chuckled. "I am not calling you out for it. There is no need to be defensive; relax."

"Speaking of relax," Audra said, "I was invited to a house party this Friday night, and I need a plus one."

"And you were thinking of me?" Kenny asked. "After you ditched me last Friday? No thanks."

"It's not far from where you live and not late at night. It's actually my cousin Wendy's party. She said she is inviting loads of single guys—right up my alley. It starts at eight. That's tame, isn't it?"

"I guess," Kenny said. "I am going to have to check with Camden to see what he is planning. I can't ditch him two Friday nights in a row. And if I'm coming, I am driving my own car so that I can leave whenever."

"Good. Great," Audra said happily. "Let me know."

Chapter Eleven

"**K**enny!" Ashton bellowed.

Kenny jumped. She had fallen asleep on the couch in Camden's office. She had moved over to the couch to get more comfortable and must have drifted off.

She blinked at Ashton. "Hey."

"I heard you were down here, and I came to say hi." Ashton grinned.

Camden scowled behind him. "I told him not to wake you up."

Kenny chuckled and stretched. "What time is it?"

"Nine-thirty," Camden said. "It took me an hour and a half to sort out the mess he made of things."

"It was an honest mistake," Ashton grinned, "but boy, did I pay for it. Not only did Camden swoop in to correct my work, but he also made sure that Uncle Jim and my father knew he was the wunderkind who did it."

Camden was irritated. "I told you not to try things your

way. I am too tired to rehash the same thing with you. And yes, I had to get our fathers involved because it is technically their big case. You had one thing to do, and you just had to try to showboat. Your ego is bigger than Tori DaSilva's butt."

"Now that's specific," Kenny grinned. "Who is Tori DaSilva?"

"A girl from prep school," Ashton replied. "I did as you said, Kenny; I went looking for girls I went to prep school with in order to write my own love story like what you and Camden have. I searched for all the girls I was friends with and found Tori DaSilva. I remember her being pretty and smart. So, I hit her up, hoping we could reconnect and be friendly."

Kenny nodded eagerly. "Cool."

"Not cool," Ashton said. "I invited her to lunch in our cafeteria, hoping it would be a neutral location where we could embark on our friendship journey."

"And?" Kenny raised an eyebrow.

"It turns out she is quite well-known to some of the men here," Ashton sighed. "My pretty and smart prep school pal is now a dancer at Sensuous City who goes by the stage name Jessica Rabbit. Apparently, it's because she is shaped like the fictional character—large boobs, wide hips, small waist, an hourglass figure."

"Except hers is obviously surgically done," Camden said.

"And sadly, she keeps in character even when she's not dancing," Ashton continued. "She wore a Jessica Rabbit-inspired outfit to lunch today—a long red dress with a slit at the front and a long red wig that matched her dress."

Camden chuckled. "Everybody kept going down to the cafeteria wondering if there was an entertainment event."

Kenny laughed. "You are making this up."

"I wish I was making it up," Ashton groaned, sitting on the couch across from Kenny. "I was just sitting there trying to have a normal conversation, but she was so committed to her 'Jessica Rabbit' persona that it was hard to take anything seriously. Camden came down to see for himself; he can tell you this is no joke."

Camden nodded. "Everybody found it funny."

"So, how did the lunch go?" Kenny asked, stifling another laugh.

"Terribly," Ashton sighed. "She kept flirting with the guys passing by, posing every five seconds. I could barely get a word in. I was hoping for a chance to catch up with an old friend, maybe rekindle something real, but... she wasn't the same person I remembered."

Kenny leaned forward, still smiling but with more understanding. "Did you get a chance to talk at all so you could get to know the real her?"

Ashton shrugged. "Not really. I tried to steer the conversation toward our old school days, but she kept brushing it off, saying that was in the past and she's 'living in the now.' Much to my chagrin, she was fully embracing the Jessica Rabbit persona, and then I found out why."

"Why?" Kenny and Camden asked almost at once.

"Because she thought I was paying her for her performance. She said when she heard 'lunch at Byfield and Byfield,' that was her conclusion. She usually does bachelor parties, she said, but never a regular lunch at an office."

Kenny's eyes widened in disbelief, and Camden covered his mouth, trying not to burst out laughing again.

"Wait, wait, hold on," Kenny said, his laughter barely contained. "She thought you hired her for... a lunch performance?"

Ashton nodded, grimacing. "Yup. She said she figured it was one of those upscale corporate lunch gigs, so she showed up ready to 'entertain.' She was even waiting for me to pay her at the end of it."

Camden finally lost it, laughing so hard he had to wipe tears from his eyes. "You can't make this up, Ashton! This is the most ridiculous thing I've ever heard."

"I know!" Ashton threw his hands up in the air. "I was sitting there in the middle of the cafeteria, surrounded by my coworkers, trying to have a genuine conversation, and she's out there thinking she's at an event. I had no idea how to explain to her that this was just... lunch! This is going to be a legend around here for years. People were taking photos, probably thinking I hired her for some office stunt."

"Luckily, we cleared up the misunderstanding," Ashton said. "I paid her for her services, and we agreed that we would one day laugh about it."

"Hey, not every reconnection is going to lead to a love story," Kenny said. "But it's a start. You're putting yourself out there."

"True," Ashton nodded. "I arranged to meet Tori later. I made it clear it was her and not Jessica Rabbit that I wanted to see."

He looked at his watch. "I'll have to go; she comes off her shift at twelve."

Shortly after he exited, Lorraine Byfield pushed her head around the door. "Oh good, honey, you are here! I brought food."

"Oh, thanks, Mom," Camden said.

"Kenny!" She looked at Kenny, a pleased smile on her face. "I didn't know you were here too. How are you, lovely?"

Kenny smiled. It was always a genuine pleasure to

see Lorraine Byfield. She was sweetness and warmth personified, wrapped up in a petite package. Lorraine was in her early fifties, tall and leggy, with wavy brown hair and gray eyes.

Lorraine hugged her. She smelled good, as usual.

"I stopped by to take dinner for Jim and Camden. I didn't know you were here, but luckily I have enough food for two. Bon appétit, children."

"Cool," Camden breathed. "I am hungry! I should be carb-stacking for my race on Sunday, but I keep forgetting to eat. Thanks, Mom."

"I could eat too," Kenny said. "Thanks, Lorraine." She took the bag from Lorraine and rummaged in it. "Oh, good heavens! Lasagna and garlic bread! You're a saint, Lorraine."

Lorraine laughed, a soft, melodic sound that always made Kenny feel at ease. "You know me, always making sure my family is fed. I'll leave you two to it." She gave them both another warm smile and headed for the door. "By the way, Camden, I had an awful dream about you the other night."

Camden raised his eyebrows. "Not one of those again. My mother puts more emphasis on dreams than regular people."

Lorraine sighed. "I do, but you must admit sometimes my dreams are accurate and legitimate."

"Well, what was it this time?" Camden asked.

"I dreamt that you got into an accident at your cycling event," Lorraine said worriedly. "Please wear your helmet and be safe."

"Thanks, Mom, I will be safe," Camden said. "And thanks for the food."

Lorraine left them, and Camden and Kenny turned their attention to the food. The comforting smell of lasagna and garlic bread filled the room, momentarily pushing aside any lingering thoughts of Lorraine's dream.

Kenny took a hearty bite of the lasagna and sighed in contentment. "I didn't know I needed this lasagna in my life. Your mom really outdid herself this time."

"She always does," Camden agreed, grabbing a piece of garlic bread. "Even if she's got a knack for worrying a bit too much."

Kenny chuckled. "I'd say that's just part of her charm. I mean, mothers worry—that's just what they do."

"Yeah," Camden said, nodding. "Her dreams do tend to be accurate, though. Maybe I shouldn't race. I am not prepared. I haven't been training and tapering; my nutrition is lacking. I should be carbing up, hitting the gym, doing some interval training for endurance. I am going to come dead last."

Kenny chuckled. "It's a short circuit; you're doing it for charity. Just stay focused on the race and enjoy it. Half of the people entering are in the same boat anyway."

Camden nodded. "True. But it's only fitting that, as president of the club, I should at least be ranked in the top twenty."

Kenny smirked, taking a bite of his lasagna. "Ranked in the top twenty? You're aiming high for someone who's already talking themselves out of it."

"Well, I've got to make a good impression," Camden replied, a hint of a grin creeping in. "Can't let the president be the one dragging behind the pack. What kind of example is that?"

"Exactly," Kenny said, pointing at him with his fork. "So, stop doubting yourself. You've done races before; you'll be fine. Plus, it's not like your mom's dream was all doom and gloom, right? Maybe she just wants you to be cautious."

Camden leaned back, sighing. "Yeah, but you know how it is with her. Whenever she dreams about something, it's like a weird, cryptic warning."

"Maybe the warning's just that you need to relax," Kenny said with a grin. "Get out of your head and ride for fun. After all, it's supposed to be enjoyable."

Camden cracked a smile. "You're right. I'll just focus on finishing the race, having fun, and... not embarrassing myself."

"Exactly. Whatever you do, I'll be waiting for you at the finish line. I'll try to wear sexy lingerie."

Camden laughed. "Now that's motivation I can get behind."

"Before I forget," Kenny said, "I am invited to a party with Audra this Friday night."

"I hate that Audra is taking over our weekends," Camden grumbled.

Kenny laughed. "Somehow, I knew you'd say that, even though it's just two weekends in a couple of hundred that I am hanging out with someone other than you."

"I know," Camden said. "I'll probably have to work late anyway."

"You see," Kenny said, "I would have been home alone."

"No, I would carry the work home," Camden said. "You would know that I am in my home office; we'd be in the same space."

"Nah, I think I am looking forward to the party," Kenny grinned.

"Have fun, but not too much," Camden said.

Chapter Twelve

Wendy's house party was by the poolside of her newly renovated home. Kenny had gotten directions from Audra and showed up promptly at eight. She parked behind a long line of cars leading up to the house, wanting to leave whenever she pleased without getting blocked in.

Thankfully, she had worn wedges—the walk up the steep incline to Wendy's place was not meant for fancy shoes. She passed Audra's car on her way up to the house and stopped. Her friend was sitting inside, talking on the phone.

Audra rolled down the window and grinned when she saw Kenny. "I was waiting for you. When you said you were three minutes away, I sat in here and passed the time talking to my aunt on the phone."

"Why do you always manage to look so good? Red is your color."

Kenny glanced down at her red peplum blouse and black pants, then smiled. "Thank you. Camden said I looked nice and demure at the front." She turned around, showing Audra the V-neckline at the back. "And vampish at the back. He almost didn't let me leave the house—he's developing a possessive streak. I think I like it."

"Show off," Audra snorted. "But then again, you and Camden were kind of expected to be together when we were younger. It was supposed to be Rory, me, you, and Camden. We'd get married and live beside each other."

"And comb each other's hair," Kenny chuckled.

Audra laughed. "We had no idea what we were talking about back then."

"I think Camden and I are going to break up," Kenny said, slowing down.

"Why?" Audra asked, surprised.

"We have a month left before the ultimatum runs out. He doesn't seem like a man contemplating marriage."

"What would that even look like, though?" Audra asked.

"I don't know," Kenny replied, "but everyone I've talked to who got married knew it was coming. They had conversations about where they wanted to do it, how many people they'd invite, where to get the ring—it was always a done deal."

"But everybody's story is different," Audra said. "I had a colleague who proposed to another colleague in the middle of a heart operation."

"What?" Kenny chuckled.

"And my aunt Venna—my dad's sister—the one everybody thought would be alone forever? She went on a cruise and came back married. Her guy proposed on the spur of the moment over drinks one night. The whole family thought it wouldn't last, but they'll be celebrating ten years in a couple of months."

Kenny nodded. "My situation is more nuanced than that.

We live together. I want some indication that a proposal is coming."

"It will come," Audra assured her. "Camden's not stupid. I figure that's why he's going all caveman on you. He's thinking, 'That's my wife.'"

Kenny giggled. "I hope so."

"I know so," Audra said confidently.

They reached the side gate to the pool area and were stopped by security.

"Your name, please?" the security guard asked.

Audra looked at Kenny and laughed. "Why is Wendy so extra?"

"Your whole family is extra," Kenny responded, grinning.

"My name is Audra Beckles, and this here is my plus-one, Kenny Carter."

The security guard checked his list, nodded, and let them through. "Have a good evening."

"Thanks," they both said in unison.

The poolside was beautifully lit, with twinkling string lights draped across the palm trees, casting a soft glow over the scene. Tables with crisp white linens were set up, and a bar at one end was already buzzing with guests mingling. Soft music played in the background, and the scent of ocean air mixed with the faint aroma of grilled food wafted from a nearby barbecue station.

"This is gorgeous," Kenny said, looking around. "Wendy went all out."

Audra smiled, slipping her arm through Kenny's. "She always does. You know how she is—nothing is halfway with my cousin."

They found a small table near the pool's edge, where the water shimmered with reflections from the lights. As they sat down, Kenny's phone buzzed with a text from Camden.

She glanced at it quickly and sighed.

"What is it?" Audra asked, raising an eyebrow.

Kenny hesitated, then showed her the screen. "Just him asking if I got here alright."

"That's husband behavior right there," Audra said. "Then again, some husbands wouldn't care."

"You're giving me too much hope," Kenny said, sipping her drink.

"Camden is almost ready to pop the big question; he just wants to do it his way. Trust me. I know Camden's type—he's already planning something. Men like him don't let good things slip away."

Kenny smiled, though it didn't quite reach her eyes. "I guess, we'll see."

Before Audra could respond, a server approached their table with two champagne flutes. "Compliments of the host," she said, setting them down.

"Wendy," Audra muttered, shaking her head but smiling. "Always the hostess."

They clinked glasses, but just as Kenny was about to take a sip, she saw Ashton entering the party from the opposite side of the pool with a woman clinging to his arm. He looked hunted.

"As I live and breathe," Kenny choked with laughter. "Just yesterday, Ashton was talking about the woman he's here with cosplaying as Jessica Rabbit and embarrassing him at work. And now here she is... in the same Rabbitish outfit. I wonder why."

Audra looked around, and her eyes widened. "Oh wow. She's... er... bodacious and curvaceous."

"Camden says it's enhanced," Kenny whispered.

"I need to find out who her surgeon is," Audra said. "I want some of that."

"Really?" Kenny asked. "You want melon-sized tits and a rear that looks like a hump? She looks like a girl centaur—all she needs is a tail to complete the totally weird-looking behind."

"Yes, I want to look like a girl centaur," Audra nodded. "Look at all the stares she's getting."

"Because she's half-naked," Kenny snorted. "Just one sneeze, and her tits would jump right out of that top."

"Don't be jealous, Kenny," Audra teased. "I bet that's the reason Ashton went back to her—he couldn't resist seeing if a sneeze would make that top go flying. I bet you he's waving black pepper under her nose every two seconds."

Kenny almost choked with laughter. "I hope you're not serious," she finally said after catching her breath.

"Only half serious," Audra said, turning back around. "I'm just tired of being stick-thin. I wish I weren't so much of an ectomorph."

"You are crazy," Kenny said. "You have the model look."

"Without the height," Audra snorted. "Pretty soon, my eight-year-old son is going to be taller than I am."

"And here we go," Kenny said. "Let's not spend the rest of the evening moaning about our looks or height. Tell me about Jairo instead."

"I can't," Audra said.

"You had better," Kenny glared at her. "I won't judge you."

"I am shameless when it comes to him," Audra said. "I have always been."

"Tell me the history," Kenny said, "and why I haven't heard of him before."

"The potted version," Audra sighed. "His mother won the lottery and moved him and his sisters next door to us. I was thirteen, and he was seventeen. The cutest boy I had ever seen."

"He is good-looking," Kenny said. "Dark skin and light eyes are always a striking combination."

Audra nodded. "But more than that, he was intelligent and treated me with a slight disdain that I found intriguing."

Kenny laughed.

"By then, he was somewhat famous locally," Audra said. "He was the top striker for his school in the schoolboy football competition. Not only did he help Greenland High win the DaCosta Cup that year, but he was also playing in some Premier League games and was killing it. If you followed football, you would have known about him."

"Never heard of him," Kenny said. "And what's more, you didn't tell me a thing."

"I secretly liked him but pretended that I didn't," Audra said. "He was my secret crush. Besides, he left Jamaica when he was nineteen and went to play for the English Premier League. His mother sold the house next door and migrated to Canada. I didn't give him a thought until I saw him in Kingston, my second year in med school. He was out here on vacation. We had a thing."

"You mean you had sex." Kenny leaned forward. "He took your virginity."

"It was more like I gave it to him," Audra said. "And then we broke up. There was no future for us—we were on different trajectories. It wasn't going to happen. In my third year of med school, he came out here again, and we reconnected. And we did the same dance: passionate sex and then a breakup."

Kenny nodded. "I remember thinking you were in something with someone."

"Yup, it was him," Audra nodded. "I heard he was out here in the fourth and final year of med school. He didn't contact me as he usually did. I found out why when I read on the internet that he was engaged to be married and his big splashy wedding was going to be in St. Ann, where his fiancée was from. I don't know what got into me…"

"Jealousy? Envy?" Kenny raised her eyebrows.

"Something like that," Audra said. "I conveniently bumped into him in the hotel lobby where I knew he usually stayed. It was the night of his bachelor party. We had one last tussle between the sheets, and we agreed never to see each other again because we obviously couldn't help ourselves, etcetera, etcetera. I got pregnant, and he got married. And we didn't see each other again until the other night."

"Where you had sex again?" Kenny asked.

"Yes," Audra said. "I told you I was shameless. I need to build up my resistance to him."

"And he to you," Kenny said. "Why didn't his marriage survive?"

"I have no clue," Audra shrugged. "Jairo and I don't really have meaningful conversations. We see each other, and we get horizontal."

"So he doesn't know about Jason?" Kenny asked.

"Nope," Audra said. "And I'm not sure I'll tell him. I may never see him again."

"Pathetic," Kenny snorted.

"I thought you weren't going to judge," Audra said.

"I'm not judging you," Kenny protested. "All I'm saying is they both deserve to know about each other. At least if Jairo shows no interest in his son when Jason grows up, you can say you told his father about him, and he wasn't interested. Personally, I think every kid should have a father. My dad was great—before he died, all five of us would tell you we were his favorite. I sometimes find myself missing my dad so badly, even though he died seventeen years ago."

"You have a point," Audra said.

"But you will not tell him," Kenny said. "You and Jairo will go on using each other for sex; no relationship required."

"I won't be seeing him again," Audra said.

"Rubbish," Kenny snorted. "You will. You'll probably be playing hopscotch in and out of his bed until you can't open your legs any longer."

Audra hooted with laughter. "I can actually picture myself old and crotchety and unable to open my legs."

"Ladies!" Wendy exuberantly greeted them. She kissed them on both cheeks and gave them a hug. "I'm sorry I'm so late in coming over. I had a little consult with my physiotherapist." Wendy pointed to her bandaged ankle. "It's acting up again. It's a good thing I invited her."

Kenny looked over Wendy's shoulder and saw Jody.

Same characters, different Friday night, she thought darkly.

They chitchatted with Wendy, who borrowed Audra for a minute. Kenny sat at the table and looked around. Her eyes connected with Ashton's as if he were willing her to look at him.

He smiled a slow, pleased smile and came over to her, slipping into Audra's seat.

"Kenny, are you stalking me?"

"Nope," Kenny smiled, "small town."

"Remember Tori DaSilva, aka Jessica Rabbit, the girl I was telling you about?"

"Yes," Kenny nodded.

"Well, she's here with me. She slipped away to the bathroom for a little."

"I saw when you two came in," Kenny said. "I thought she was done with the cosplaying and was going to be normal."

"I thought so, too," Ashton said. "But she came over to my place just when I was leaving. I don't know how she found my address. I feel like I'm being hunted."

Kenny chuckled. "So why did you come with her to the party?"

"She drove behind me," Ashton leaned toward Kenny. "Then, when I walked up here, she grabbed my arms. I told the security at the side gate that she wasn't with me, and he didn't even listen—he was so busy drooling at her fake tits. So, here I am."

Kenny laughed.

Tori came over and looped her arms around Ashton.

"Ashton, darling, this party is boring."

Ashton tried to shrug off her arms, but she clamped down on his shoulders with her talon-like fingernails.

"Tori, we are not going anywhere together. My girlfriend here will not be pleased."

Tori straightened up and glared at Kenny. "You are his girlfriend?"

"It appears so," Kenny said, deciding to bail out Ashton, who was looking obviously uncomfortable.

"He went out with me the other day," Tori said, pushing herself away from Ashton. "He said he was single. You're lying."

"She is not!" Ashton sputtered. "I am very much in love with Kenny!"

"That's a boy's name," Tori looked at Kenny suspiciously. "Why would a girl be named Kenny? Are you transgender?"

"I beg your pardon?" Kenny asked.

"Never mind," Tori muttered. "I can tell you're a woman."

"Thank God for that," Kenny chuckled.

"You'll have to fight me for him," Tori shrugged. "I set my sights on Ashton. He is mine."

Kenny raised an eyebrow, smirking. "Fight you for him? Please, honey, I'm not in the business of fighting over men."

Tori crossed her arms, narrowing her eyes. "I am, and I always get what I want."

Ashton shifted uncomfortably. "Tori, stop. I told you—I'm with Kenny. What we had was... well, whatever it was, it's over."

Tori scoffed, looking between the two of them. "We had a lot more than 'whatever.' Don't act like you didn't enjoy it. I don't just give blow jobs for free."

Kenny glanced at Ashton, who now looked like he wanted the ground to swallow him.

"Look, Tori," Kenny said, trying not to laugh, "whatever happened between you and Ashton is in the past. But right now, he's with me. And if he wanted to be with you, he would be. The fact that he isn't should tell you everything you need to know."

Tori stared at Kenny for a moment, then turned her gaze back to Ashton, who still hadn't said much beyond a few awkward protests. She sneered, clearly not getting the response she wanted, and flipped her hair over her shoulder.

"You'll regret this, Ashton," she said coldly. "When you come crawling back, don't expect me to be waiting. I move on fast."

With that, she turned on her heels and strutted off, her stilettos clicking loudly against the ground as she disappeared into the crowd.

There was a long silence as both Kenny and Ashton watched her leave. Then, finally, Ashton let out a long breath. "Well, that was... intense and oddly embarrassing. By the way, she's the one who insisted on the blow job. It takes a strong man to say no to a pushy woman who's intent on pleasing him."

Kenny chuckled, shaking her head. "You sure know how to pick them."

Ashton winced. "Yeah, I think I need to work on that."

Kenny smirked. "No kidding. You owe me big time for that little performance."

"Trust me, I know," Ashton said with a sheepish grin. "If you ever need any legal help, I'm available free of charge for whatever reason."

Kenny laughed. "I'm going to need you to put that in writing."

Ashton nodded. "You are a shrewd woman." He wrote on a napkin, 'I owe you, Kenny, for personal services rendered. A million times thank you for saving me.'

He handed it to her.

Kenny chuckled. "You didn't sign it."

Ashton shook his head. "You are shrewd."

"And date it, too," Kenny said.

"My God, are you sure you didn't go to law school?" Ashton grumbled.

Kenny laughed heartily, quite oblivious to the fact that Jody was watching her interaction with Ashton. Her fists clenched, and her eyes narrowed.

****

The night passed relatively drama-free after that. Kenny chatted and laughed with different groups of people, but by eleven, she was struggling to hold in her yawns.

"I'm going to bounce," she said to Audra.

"Me too," Audra said. "Most of Wendy's single guy friends are falling all over themselves to talk to Tori. I asked her who her surgeon was, and she said it's all-natural."

Kenny laughed. "I'm happy she didn't tell you."

"I want to join the sisterhood of curves," Audra pouted. "Why do you people have a problem with bodily enhancements?"

"When it looks exaggerated and fake, it's off-putting. In my opinion, subtle enhancements aren't bad, but Tori's is too much," Kenny said, looking around. "Where's Wendy? I need to say goodbye."

"Over there. I might as well come with you," Audra said.

They left shortly after saying their goodbyes.

Kenny didn't notice that Ashton came after her, too. She hadn't spoken to him much after the little scene with Tori.

"Hey, Kenny!" he called after her when they were nearing Audra's car.

Kenny stopped and looked around. Ashton caught up to her.

"What the..." she didn't get to ask as Ashton grabbed her and kissed her.

Before Kenny could respond, he let her go.

Kenny blinked rapidly. "What the hell?" she whispered.

"Play along," Ashton urged. "She's following."

"You owe me again," Kenny said. "Big time. I don't see why you're so afraid of one woman."

"Because she's crazy. A little too crazy for me, and I don't mind crazy at all," Ashton whispered.

They heard a car door slam, followed by the screech of tires as a car pulled away.

"That's her," Ashton sighed. "Gone. Hopefully forever."

Audra laughed behind them. "That was some demonstration."

"I had to do it," Ashton chuckled. "Please don't tell Camden on me. I know he'll bust a gasket if he hears I kissed you."

"Oh, I'll definitely tell him," Kenny said. "Camden and I don't keep secrets from each other, and tonight is too juicy not to share."

"Then I'll prepare to be punched on Monday." Ashton

grinned. "Thanks again, Kenny. You're a real one."

"See you on Sunday," Audra said, opening her car door. "I'm coming to your cycle club thingy to cheer on Camden."

Chapter Thirteen

It was shaping up to be a superb Sunday morning for racing. Camden inhaled the early morning air with anticipation. They were using the Montego Bay Sports Complex as their venue. The event would start at nine, but he had to be there at seven with the organizing committee.

"How is it going?" Jody asked, tapping his shoulder. He was checking and double-checking his bicycle.

"Fine. Great. It is going to be a good day," Camden answered, straightening up.

"Yep," Jody smiled.

"You are looking pretty today," Camden complimented her with a smile. She really did look good. She was dressed in a fitted navy blue polo shirt embroidered with the event's logo, Ride or Die, and a pair of slim black jeans. Her hair was pulled back into a sleek ponytail, and her sunglasses rested on top of her head, giving her an effortlessly cool vibe. The sunlight caught the faint shimmer of her lip gloss as she smiled, adding to her radiance.

"Thanks," Jody replied, a little surprised but pleased by the compliment. "Figured I'd at least try to look like I belong here since I'm not participating."

"You fit in just fine," Camden said, giving her a wink. "Besides, you make this whole thing run smoothly. We couldn't do it without you."

Jody blushed slightly, brushing a strand of hair behind her ear. "It's a team effort."

"Yeah, but you're the backbone," Camden said, glancing over at the growing activity around them as other committee members started arriving. "Seriously, I appreciate everything you've done to make this happen."

"Stop it; you're going to make me emotional before the race even starts," Jody teased, though her voice softened with sincerity.

Camden laughed. "Save the emotions for after I win."

"Confident, aren't you?" she asked, raising an eyebrow.

"Not really psyching myself up," Camden replied with a grin. "But the track isn't bad; it's a good day for racing. What could go wrong?"

Jody looked around. "Let's just hope the weather holds up. The forecast said there might be some rain later."

Camden glanced up at the sky, which was clear for now, and shrugged. "If it rains, it rains."

"So, where's your cheering squad?" Jody asked. "Is she coming to support you?"

"Of course," Camden nodded. "It's still early. Kenny loves her Sunday morning lie-ins; I'm sure she will be here. She's my loyal supporter—my actual ride or die."

Jody snorted. "I doubt that."

"What?" Camden frowned.

"I promised myself I wouldn't say anything," Jody sighed.

"I told myself I would stay out of people's business. It has nothing to do with me…"

"What are you going on about?" Camden frowned.

"This," Jody said, reaching into her pocket for her phone. She pulled it out, unlocked it, scrolled through her pictures, and handed it to Camden.

It was a video of Kenny and Ashton talking closely together as if they were whispering.

Camden was shaken. He couldn't even watch the rest of the clip. He looked at Jody.

"I can't believe this."

"Swipe right," Jody said. "There's more."

Camden swiped right. There was a picture of Kenny and Ashton in a passionate clinch.

His hands trembled as he thrust the phone back to Jody, his heart pounding in his chest. "What the hell is this?" Camden muttered, his voice low but laced with disbelief.

Jody sighed, putting her phone away, her face a mix of regret and concern. "I didn't want to be the one to show you, Cam. But I couldn't let you keep walking around like everything's fine when this is happening behind your back. I went to the house party because Wendy is my client. And then there was Kenny cozying up to this guy who has more than a passing resemblance to you."

Camden took a step back, rubbing his temples as if trying to make sense of what he'd just seen. "This can't be right."

"It is," Jody said, crossing her arms. "When I saw them at Mingles a week ago, I knew something was up. And now, Friday night? It's too much. I warned her that I would tell you, and she laughed in my face."

"She did?" Camden whispered, the words barely audible.

Jody watched him carefully. "Look, I'm sorry, Cam. I know this hurts, but you deserve to know the truth."

Camden nodded, though he felt like he was in a daze, his mind swirling with anger, confusion, and pain. Kenny, the woman he'd trusted so deeply, the one he'd called his 'ride or die,' was betraying him with Ashton. His stomach churned. His own cousin.

"I need to talk to her," Camden finally muttered, his jaw tightening.

"Don't do anything rash, okay?" Jody advised, stepping closer. "Just... take some time. Process it. You've got a big day today. Don't let this ruin it."

Camden shook his head, a bitter laugh escaping his lips. "How am I supposed to focus on racing after seeing that?"

Jody placed a hand on his arm, her eyes full of empathy. "I get it. But you've worked too hard for this, Cam. Don't let her take this from you too. Not today."

He looked at her, his emotions battling for control inside him. Part of him wanted to storm off, confront Kenny, and demand answers. But another part knew Jody was right. This race was important; he had committed to it. He couldn't just walk off at the last minute. The spectators were trickling in.

Camden exhaled sharply, nodding. "I'll focus on the race. But after today..." His voice trailed off, the weight of the situation settling over him. "I think Kenny and I are done."

Jody squeezed his arm gently. "I'm here if you need me. Whatever you decide to do."

He didn't even watch her as she walked away. His mind was racing; there had to be some explanation. Was it AI?

If it was, it was realistic—too realistic. He couldn't rest, not in his mind and surely not on his feet, as he paced up and down the track, barely acknowledging his parents, who had arrived early to cheer him on.

He made sure he was nowhere near the cheering section when Kenny arrived. He didn't feel as if he was moving in reality.

He barely acknowledged his fellow bikers as they gathered around the starting point of the track. He felt numb somewhere in the region of his heart. When the starting gun went off, he pulled out like everyone else, determined to push the pain to the back of his mind. But then, on lap two, someone from the Sorenson Bikers Club clipped his bike. If his mind had been fully focused, he could have maneuvered through that incident, but it wasn't, and he went sailing through the air, the world spinning around him in a blur. He hit the ground hard, the impact knocking the wind from his lungs. For a moment, he couldn't move, couldn't breathe. Pain radiated through his body, but the adrenaline dulled it, keeping him numb just enough to maintain his focus.

Shouts from the crowd echoed in the distance, but all Camden could hear was the rush of blood in his ears. He struggled to get up, his limbs feeling heavy and uncooperative. His bike lay a few feet away, the handlebars twisted and the wheels spinning uselessly.

"Cam!" A voice broke through the haze. Jody. She was running toward him, her face pale with worry.

"I'm fine," he grunted, even though everything hurt. His ribs, his shoulder—something was definitely wrong, but he wasn't about to admit it. Not now. Not in front of everyone.

"You're not fine," Jody said firmly, kneeling next to him. "Stay down, Cam. Don't make it worse."

But Camden shook his head, pushing himself up with shaky arms. He couldn't lie there. He needed to finish this race; he needed to prove that he could push through.

"Camden!" Jody's voice was sharper now, more insistent. "Listen to me. You need to stop."

"I can't," he muttered, stumbling to his feet. "I have to finish the race."

But as he tried to take a step toward his bike, his vision swam, and the ground tilted beneath him. The pain he'd been pushing away came roaring back, sharp and unforgiving. His legs buckled, and this time, he couldn't stop himself from falling.

Chapter Fourteen

She hated hospitals, Kenny thought, clutching Audra's hand for dear life. How did a perfect morning turn into this? Her heart had nearly stopped after seeing Camden fly over his bicycle handlebars like a ragdoll. The sight of him lying there, motionless after struggling to get up, had ripped her breath away. And now, here she was, sitting in this sterile, cold hospital waiting room, her nerves frayed to the point of snapping.

Audra squeezed Kenny's hand; her own face reflected her worry. "He's going to be okay," Audra said, but the uncertainty in her voice was clear. "Camden's strong. He'll pull through this."

Kenny nodded, though her throat was tight. How did things go so wrong? One minute, she was preparing to watch him race, and the next, she was racing to the hospital, her mind replaying the image of Camden hitting the ground over and over.

Camden's parents were already sitting in the waiting room. Lorraine and Jim looked like they had aged years since that morning. They were the ones who had rushed him to the hospital.

She hugged them both, united in their uncertainty about Camden.

"I am so happy Terrence was on duty when we got here," Lorraine said. "He immediately took over and checked Camden over."

Kenny sighed a deep sigh of relief. Terrence was a relative, a cousin of Lorraine's; he had even lived with them at one point. He was now their default family doctor since their other doctor had retired.

The door to the waiting room swung open, and Terrence stepped in, his expression unreadable. Kenny shot to her feet, her heart pounding in her chest.

"Is he… is Camden okay?" she asked, her voice trembling.

Terrence glanced down at his clipboard, then looked up, his face softening. "He's stable. He took quite a fall, and there are some fractures in his ribs and a mild concussion, but he's going to recover. He's lucky."

Kenny let out a breath she hadn't realized she was holding, tears springing to her eyes. Relief washed over her, but it was quickly followed by anxiety. "Can I see him?"

Terrence hesitated for a moment, then nodded. "You can all see him, one at a time. He's awake, but he seems a little confused. He appears to be suffering from a little amnesia."

Kenny froze, her mind struggling to process the doctor's words. Amnesia? Her heart pounded in her chest as she exchanged a glance with Lorraine and Jim. Lorraine covered her mouth with her hand, visibly shaken, while Jim stared at the floor, his fists clenched.

"Amnesia?" Kenny finally managed to say. "How... how

bad is it?"

The doctor sighed. "It's temporary, most likely. The concussion caused some short-term memory loss, but it's hard to say how much he remembers until we talk with him more. He might be confused for a little while, but we're optimistic he'll regain his memory soon."

Kenny's stomach churned.

"Who wants to go first?"

"Me," Kenny said, looking at Lorraine and Jim apologetically.

"It's fine, Kenny," Lorraine said. "I know you are worried."

"I'll take you to his room," Terrence said, motioning for her to follow.

Her legs felt like they were made of lead as she walked down the hallway. Taking a deep breath, she opened the door and stepped inside. Camden was propped up in the hospital bed, his face bruised on one side and his eyes slightly unfocused. His head turned slowly as she entered, and for a moment, there was a flicker of recognition—or was it confusion?

"Kenny," he said, his voice hoarse but soft. "What... what happened?"

Her throat tightened as she stepped closer. "You had an accident during the race. You... flew off your bicycle." Her voice wavered as she spoke, trying to keep the panic from seeping into her words.

Camden frowned, his brow furrowing as he tried to piece together the fragments of his memory. "The race... which race?" His voice trailed off as he winced, bringing a hand to his head.

Kenny sat down at the edge of his bed, her heart in her throat. "Terrence said you might not remember everything right away. But... but you're going to be okay." She reached for his hand, squeezing it gently.

Camden looked down at their hands for a moment, then back up at her, his eyes clouded with uncertainty. "Did I pass my bar exam?"

Kenny looked at him in horror. "Er… yes, you did."

He closed his eyes and then opened them again. "Where's Rory? We were supposed to go out later."

"Er, Cam," Kenny looked at Terrence and then back at Camden. "You graduated college, you work in your family's law firm, and we live together."

Camden's eyes flew open. "What?"

Camden stared at her, his confusion deepening. "Live together? I... I don't remember that." He shook his head slightly, wincing again from the motion. "Last thing I remember... I just finished law school and was waiting for my bar results, and Rory—"

Kenny's heart raced. How far back had Camden's memory gone? She glanced at Terrence, who was observing quietly from the corner of the room. His earlier warning about possible memory gaps echoed in her mind, but this felt more serious than she'd expected.

"Camden," she said softly, trying to keep her voice steady. "That was a long time ago. You passed the bar... and Rory... well, Rory is an architect now. He is married to Jewel; they have a son. As for us, we've been living together for two years now." She searched his face for any sign of recognition, but his expression remained one of disbelief and shock.

"Two years?" he repeated, his voice hoarse. "I... don't remember any of that. How can I not remember?"

Terrence stepped forward. "Camden, memory loss is a common symptom after a concussion, especially with head injuries like the one you suffered. The amnesia could be temporary, but right now, your mind is protecting you by blocking out certain memories. It's important not to force it. Let your brain heal at its own pace."

Camden's breathing quickened as he tried to take in what Terrence was saying. "So... we are together, huh?"

Kenny nodded, biting her lip as the tears threatened to spill. "Yes, Cam. We've been together. We love each other." She hesitated, afraid to overload him with too much information too quickly. "It's okay if you don't remember everything right now. We'll take it slow."

Camden leaned back against the pillows, staring up at the ceiling, his mind struggling to catch up with the life he had apparently forgotten. "I don't even know where to begin," he muttered. "It's like I'm waking up in someone else's life."

Kenny's heart broke at his words. She wished she could reach into his mind and pull those lost memories back, but for now, all she could do was be there, patient and supportive. "We'll figure it out together," she whispered, squeezing his hand again. "I'm not going anywhere."

He gave her a faint nod, though his eyes were still clouded with confusion. "I guess I'll just have to trust you on that," he said quietly.

Chapter Fifteen

Everything was harder with cracked ribs, Camden thought in frustration. Each breath came with a sharp, stabbing pain, and even the smallest movement felt like a battle. Sitting up, walking, or even laughing were torturous reminders of the accident. He gingerly adjusted his position in the chair, wincing as a fresh wave of discomfort shot through him.

He hadn't told anyone just how bad it was because he didn't want the constant fussing. Fussing was something that Kenny excelled at; she was always hovering around him. Not that he minded. He couldn't remember anything of their relationship past college, but he knew why he had chosen to have a relationship with her: she was hot and caring, and he had always known deep down that Kenny was the one.

But when had she gotten so hot, and why had he not married her yet? What was the holdup? She was working beside him on the patio, opting to work from home to take care of him.

He had loads of questions for her; unfortunately, she greeted each one with a trite answer. "You'll soon remember; the doctor said it will all come back to you, and I should not preempt it."

He wanted to argue, but even that took effort. A man was entitled to know certain details about himself. His parents and friends were equally unhelpful. He felt sleepy again.

Kenny looked over at him and smiled. She looked extra pretty when she did that. Then she tucked her hair behind her ears and went back to her computer.

"You are gorgeous," he whispered.

"Thanks, love," Kenny said. "You tell me that a lot."

"So, what kind of relationship do we have?" Camden asked. "Are we happy? How often do we have sex?"

Kenny looked up at him and laughed. "We have a great relationship. We have our times when we fuss, and then we make up. I'd say we are happy. And we have sex pretty often, mostly on weekends. We are both busy."

He smiled. "I feel so sleepy; these dratted pain pills have me snoozing my life away."

"You'll be as good as new in no time," Kenny said soothingly. "You got a pretty nasty fall, and yet here you are with just cracked ribs. Even your bruise seems to be clearing up."

"And amnesia," Camden said sleepily. "I have never met anyone who had amnesia, and here I am with it. Isn't it ironic?"

"Quite so," he heard Kenny whisper, and then he was floating along a cloud. He was snoozing his life away, and he didn't mind it.

It was the third week since the accident when he woke up feeling better. There was soreness in his rib area, but it was manageable. Kenny had started going back to work in person for a few days each week, and he was left to roam around his house. Rory came by to check on him every day, usually at lunchtime. Camden usually felt bereft when he left. At least he wasn't reluctant to give him details about his life like Kenny and his parents, who were following Terrence's advice as if he was any expert on amnesia.

"Tell me about Kenny," Camden said. "When did we move from friends to lovers?"

"Again," Rory grinned. "I told you that four times this week."

"Humor me; she won't give me details," Camden said. "Terrence has convinced them that my head will explode if anyone dares to give me any information."

"Well, five years ago," Rory said. "All you did was yap about Kenny. I jokingly said you should just date her already, and you didn't laugh back, so I took it that it was something you were contemplating. But you started dating this girl Vanessa—a nice girl, a great girl—but she wasn't Kenny, so you dumped her. But Kenny was already with someone else, a guy named Paul Virtue."

"I know him," Camden snarled. "Isn't he that investment banker?"

"Yup," Rory nodded. "And that relationship continued for two years while you flirted and slept with a fair share of girls. Then Kenny's guy got a job offer in the States, and he left her high and dry. The dust wasn't even settled on their breakup before you started hanging with her. For a full year, you pretended that you were just her friend, and then after a party here one night, you asked her to move in. She said yes, and here we are."

Camden closed his eyes, a sliver of a memory lancing him; moving in Kenny's things, laughing at her for still having her teddy bear from high school, and putting the tattered bear in the center of the bed, pulling her closer to him and whispering, "I've wanted to touch you like this since forever."

He felt her shudder. Kissing her all over. And finally joining his body to hers. It had felt like he was home.

He opened his eyes wider and stared at Rory. "I remember moving her in."

"Great!" Rory stood up. "I know it must be X-rated. You both took three days off work and spent it in bed. I don't need to imagine the details after that. You once told me that you can't get enough of Kenny; if you could drink her, you would."

Camden laughed. "My God, I can imagine myself saying that."

"You call her your ride or die," Rory added.

"So why aren't we married?" Camden asked.

"Apparently, that's your choice," Rory said cryptically. "I'm afraid I can't answer that for you."

****

"I am so happy that Camden is on the mend, and we can have lunch together again," Jewel said to Kenny. "I missed you so much."

They were sitting in Sea Grape Café, which was within walking distance from the office. They served the best burgers, fries, and milkshakes, and Kenny and Jewel liked to indulge at least once a month.

Kenny smiled. "I missed you too."

"No, you didn't," Jewel scowled. "You have Audra now. She is back, and the two of you are back to being besties."

"I have two besties," Kenny said. "I love you both. I would never want to choose."

Jewel grinned. "Good. I almost believe you."

Kenny laughed. "Do you know what today is?"

"No," Jewel shook her head.

"Ultimatum day," Kenny said. "Today would have been the day when Camden would have decided if he would marry me. I imagine it both ways: him saying, 'I am sorry, Kenny, but we have run our course,' or 'Kenny, will you marry me?' But instead, he has lost his memories, and I am in limbo."

Jewel's eyes softened as she reached across the table to squeeze Kenny's hand. "I can't imagine how hard that must be for you. Are you okay?"

Kenny sighed, looking down at their intertwined hands. "Honestly, I don't know. Part of me was relieved because it gave us more time. But another part of me feels like I've been robbed of a moment I needed—good or bad."

"Have you talked to him about it?" Jewel asked gently.

Kenny shook her head. "No. How can I? He doesn't even remember the relationship we had. I don't want to pressure him. I don't want him to feel obligated just because of who we used to be."

"And what if his memory doesn't come back?" Jewel asked.

"Don't say that," Kenny gasped. "Don't even think it."

"Sorry," Jewel shrugged. "Just pointing out a possibility."

"Terrence said his brain is probably protecting him from something. What the hell could it be?" Kenny fretted.

"There you are!" Jody growled from behind them. "I knew it was you."

Kenny groaned. "Hello, Jody."

Jody pulled up a chair and sat down uninvited. "You are keeping Camden away from his real friends. I demand to see him."

"When he is okay enough to see you, he can," Kenny said. "He doesn't remember the cycling club or anything from the past five years. I sent you all an email."

"Liar," Jody growled. "You are keeping him away from me, especially because you know that I know."

"What on earth are you talking about?" Kenny frowned.

"I saw you kissing Ashton at Wendy's party a couple of weeks ago," Jody said. "I showed the video to Camden."

Jewel gasped.

Kenny looked at her friend. "It was nothing. I'll tell you about the whole thing later. To be honest, I'd forgotten about that incident with Ashton. It's actually hilarious."

"Hilarious?" Jody shook her head. "You are a piece of work, Kenny. I am going to figure out a way to get through to Camden. You have him hostage while you're cheating on him."

Kenny opened her mouth to protest and then thought better of it. "Jody, have you ever thought that you are jumping to the wrong conclusions about me because you've always wanted to break up my relationship with Camden?"

"I can't believe you can sit here calmly acting all innocent while you cheat on Camden. You know what he said when I showed him the video? He said, 'Kenny and I are done after this.' I bet you don't want his memory to come back."

Kenny took a deep breath, her patience thinning but still holding on. "Jody, if Camden said that, it's because he didn't know the context, and I'm not going to play into your manipulations. You've wanted to drive a wedge between us for years, and frankly, I'm tired of it."

Jody leaned forward, her eyes narrowing. "You can say whatever you want, Kenny, but the truth always comes out. You've been hiding behind Camden's memory loss, pretending to be the perfect girlfriend while sneaking around."

"Enough, Jody," Jewel interjected sharply. "Camden's been through enough, and Kenny is doing everything to help him. Stop trying to make this worse."

Jody smirked but didn't back down. "We'll see how things unfold once he remembers everything. You can't keep this façade up forever, Kenny."

Kenny exhaled, her hands clenched under the table. "I'm not keeping anything up. I'm here for Camden, whether his memory comes back or not. And when it does, we'll deal with things, but not like this. Not with your drama."

Jody stood up abruptly, knocking her chair back. "Fine. But remember, I'll be there when it all crumbles."

She stormed out, leaving a tense silence behind.

Jewel rubbed Kenny's arm gently. "Don't let her get to you."

Kenny nodded though her mind raced. "I wish Camden would remember everything... but maybe not that kiss with Ashton." She glanced at Jewel with a weak laugh. "It really was nothing. He wanted to get rid of some girl following him, and he told her I was his girlfriend. Audra was right there. What if this is the reason why Camden is not remembering the past?"

"Ah," Jewel murmured, "that would make a lot of sense."

"When he remembers, this is going to get dicey," Kenny sighed dramatically. "I wish I could turn back time and tell Camden about the whole scenario. Yes, he would be mad; he thinks Ashton is out to steal me from him, but at least he wouldn't be mad at me."

"So now I am torn—should I want him to get back his memory?"

"You are in a right pickle," Jewel declared, holding up a pickle from her burger, "but you will sort things out. I am sure of it."

Chapter Sixteen

It was raining when Camden tentatively drove to the office. Sitting in the house, watching movies and struggling not to panic because he couldn't remember important chunks of his life was getting to him. He felt like an imposter in his own life. He needed to get out. Maybe something would jog his memory. Ridgeview was midway between Montego Bay and Trelawny. The route from the house felt unfamiliar to him. When he told his father he was thinking of stopping by, he had to give him directions.

They had moved into a new building. That was information that he should have known.

His father had asked him if he was sure that he should come in. "Trust me, Camden, everybody understands that you need time to recover your memories."

What his father meant to say was, "Don't bother to come in. Nobody has the time to hold your hand and explain things to you."

This memory loss was frustrating. He could quite inexplicably remember some random information, like Kenny cutting her hair and asking him his thoughts on it, or Kenny baking sweet potato cake and them demolishing the whole tin, or Kenny and him making love in the broom closet at one of his friends' parties, but he couldn't remember major things like buying a house, his new car, or any of the cases in his career.

His father had said he was an above-average lawyer, and they were anticipating great things from him. He didn't feel like an above average anything right now. He felt lost. Kenny had to help him with everything, including opening his phone. He had studied his messages, looked at the pictures, and felt like he was spying on someone else.

He felt less alone when Kenny was with him. She had a calming effect on his life and an exciting effect as well. He absolutely knew why he had asked her to move in with him: He was in love with her. That was one thing he hadn't forgotten and the only thing that felt real. Rory was right; he had been in love with Kenny for years now.

But love wasn't enough to fill in the gaps in his mind. It was like living in someone else's skin, trying to piece together a puzzle with missing edges.

Pulling into the parking lot of the new office building, Camden turned off the car and sat there, watching the rain smear across the windshield. The building was sleek, modern, and utterly unfamiliar. How was he going to wing this?

He checked his phone, a habit that seemed ingrained even though he couldn't recall half the contacts stored in it. A message from Kenny flashed on the screen: "Are you okay?"

She must have sensed his anxiety all the way across town. Somehow, she always did.

'Yeah. Just about to head into the office,' he typed back, though his hands trembled slightly. He stared at the message for a moment before hitting send.

Gathering himself, he stepped out of the car and made his way to the entrance. The automatic doors slid open with a quiet hiss, welcoming him into a polished lobby that might as well have been a foreign country. People he vaguely recognized nodded at him as he passed, their expressions warm but wary. Were they sizing him up? Wondering if he could still handle the job? He couldn't blame them. He wasn't sure either.

"Camden," a familiar voice called out. His father stood at the far end of the lobby, his suit crisp, his face unreadable. "You made it."

"Yes," Camden replied, trying to keep his voice steady. "I made it."

His father gestured for him to follow. "Let's head to your office. We need to talk."

His office was on the second floor. The walk from the elevator felt like moving through a dream—one where every door and corridor was both familiar and strange.

His office was large, meticulously organized, and completely impersonal except for a picture of him and Kenny on the desk. They were on a mountaintop, staring at each other, leaning on a bicycle. He scanned the space, hoping for some kind of recognition, but nothing came.

"We've given you time, Camden," his father began, closing the door behind them. "But the truth is, we're running out of it. The firm needs you back fully. You were integral in a high-stakes case we are looking at. Your input has been invaluable. Noel and I have been discussing your work ethic. You are a notch above your cousins for the junior partnership position."

Junior partnership? Camden widened his eyes. Oh wow.

Jim sighed and gestured to Camden's chair. "Have a seat."

Camden sat down.

"How does it feel?" Jim asked.

"Like a regular chair," Camden said.

"I mean, isn't there a flash of light, a tumbling of ideas, a hint of recognition?"

"No, I'm trying," Camden said, the frustration bubbling up. "But I can't just… snap my fingers and make everything come back."

His father sighed and sat across from him. "I know. I promised Terrence and your mother that I wouldn't push. I don't want you to feel overwhelmed. Terrence even stressed that trying to remember can be counterproductive."

Camden nodded. "I can agree with that. Whenever I will myself to remember, I feel exhausted."

"Maybe you could review some of your old cases and get familiar with the firm's current projects. Ashton can help you with that."

"When did he start working here again?" Camden asked, wincing as a piercing pain hit his shoulder cuff.

"Three years ago," his father said. "I can't imagine what you are going through."

"Uh-huh," Camden moaned.

"What's wrong?" his father asked.

"My shoulders," Camden groaned. "I stopped taking the pain meds and decided to bear it like a man. They were making me too drowsy."

"You need a physiotherapist," Jim said. "And you need to see Terrence about prescribing something for the pain that won't make you drowsy."

Camden nodded. "I wonder if he can see me today?"

"Of course, he can," Jim said. "His office is right across

the street. Let me call him and tell him to expect you."

"I want to go through the files," Camden said.

"You are no good to us while you are in pain," Jim said. "Come on, I'll walk with you to the Medical Center."

****

Knowing you, Camden, I should have expected that you would stop taking your medication without my permission."

Camden smiled half-heartedly. Terrence was in his early forties, his mother's nephew, his childhood tormentor, and now, apparently, his doctor. His previous doctor had migrated to the UK. Of course, he knew none of this because he couldn't remember a thing. He couldn't remember switching to Terrence.

"The good news is," Terrence said, "your shoulder is healing well despite your stubbornness. But the bad news is, you're pushing yourself too hard, too fast." Terrence crossed his arms, his brow furrowed. "Skipping pain medication isn't a sign of strength, Camden. It's a tool to help your recovery, not a crutch."

Camden leaned back in the chair, wincing as his shoulder throbbed with a dull ache. "I don't like how the meds make me feel. It's like I'm walking through a fog. I can't think clearly, and I'm already having enough trouble remembering anything from the last five years."

Terrence nodded. "I get it. No one likes that feeling, but you've got to trust the process. Your body needs time, and so does your mind. Pain only complicates things. You're healing physically, but if you're in constant discomfort, it's going to make everything harder, including regaining your memories."

Camden rubbed his temple. "I feel like I'm fighting two

battles at once—my mind and my body. I just want to feel normal again."

Terrence sighed. "You're not the first person to deal with this, and you won't be the last. There are people who've come out on the other side stronger. You can, too."

"You sound like Kenny," Camden muttered, a faint smile tugging at his lips.

"Smart woman," Terrence said, scribbling something on his notepad. "She's right. And she's in your corner, as am I. You need to take it one step at a time. Maybe start with the pain meds, and we'll figure out a better dosage if they're making you too foggy. And I'm setting you up with a physiotherapist—no arguments. You need to focus on healing, both inside and out. You are familiar with this therapist; she's a part of your Cycle Club and has been harassing me about you. Her office is on the other side of the building. Her name is Jody Levy—sound familiar?"

"Nope," Camden said.

Terrence tore off the paper and handed it to him. "The pharmacy is next door. Get your meds. See Jody today if you can."

"Okay," Camden didn't argue. He was tired of fighting, tired of resisting help. "Alright," he conceded. "I'll take the meds and see the physio. But don't expect me to enjoy it."

Terrence chuckled. "I don't care if you enjoy it. I just care that you get better."

Chapter Seventeen

After visiting the pharmacy, Camden made his way to the physiotherapist's office. He was feeling a smidge better, having taken the painkiller at the pharmacy.

"Do I need to make an appointment to see Jody Levy?" Camden asked the receptionist.

She was staring at him with her mouth half-open.

"No, you don't," she recovered after a while. "I'll just tell her you're out here. She'll be quite happy to see you. How are you, by the way?"

"Feeling a little banged up," Camden replied. "Do we know each other?"

"We do," the lady nodded. "Quite well, but Kenny has been updating us, and we understand that you have amnesia."

"When you say us," Camden asked, "Who exactly are you talking about?"

"Oh, sorry," she said sheepishly. "The Cycle Club. Let me just call Jody; she'll be so happy you're here."

And she was. Camden felt guilty when the statuesque woman with a bright smile and athletic build appeared from the back, her excitement palpable. Camden's stomach was knotted with guilt as he realized he didn't recognize her at all.

"Camden!" she exclaimed, coming forward to hug him. She pulled back, scanning his face. "You look better than I expected, considering everything you've been through."

He forced a smile. "Thanks. I'm feeling... a little better."

Jody tilted her head slightly as if studying him. "Kenny's been giving the Cycle Club group regular updates about you. I wanted to see you for myself. I don't exactly trust that she is taking the best care of you, as she claims."

"You don't?" Camden was confused.

"Forget I said that," Jody said. "How's the shoulder?"

Camden rubbed it instinctively. "Still painful. That's why I'm here. Terrence insisted on it."

"Good. That shoulder needs attention. I saw when you fell on it; I thought it would have been much worse." Jody gestured toward the treatment room. "Come on back, and we'll get started. It might take a few sessions to see real progress, but I'm here for the long haul. Just like the old days."

Camden nodded, even though the old days she referred to were a blank slate to him. As he followed her into the room, the knot in his stomach tightened. "When you say the old days, what exactly do you mean?" he asked.

"You injured your hamstring three years ago," Jody said. "I was your therapist."

"Oh," Camden said. "I don't remember that."

"No worries," Jody motioned for him to sit on the padded table. "I'm going to start by assessing the range of motion in your shoulder. We'll take it slow, but don't hesitate to tell me if anything hurts more than usual."

He nodded again, watching as she prepared to begin. As her hands moved to his shoulder, expertly manipulating the joint, Camden wondered how well they actually knew each other.

"I know it's tough," Jody said softly, her tone compassionate, almost intimate. "Not remembering everything. But I'm sure you'll be fine soon. How is Kenny really treating you?"

"Great. Fine." Camden closed his eyes, focusing on the sensation in his shoulder and the steady rhythm of her voice.

"I think she is probably happy you can't remember a thing," Jody murmured, "and milking your memory loss so that she can delay answering for her crimes against you."

"Hold up," Camden looked at Jody. "What crimes against me?"

"She was cheating on you with your cousin Ashton. I even caught them on video. I showed you the clip, and you said you were going to break up with her. The accident made that impossible."

"Oh God," Camden groaned, a sharp pain hitting him out of nowhere in his head.

Camden clutched his head; the sudden pain nearly blinded him. He squeezed his eyes shut, trying to breathe through the sharp wave of agony.

"Camden, are you okay?" Jody's voice softened immediately, her hands pulling back from his shoulder.

He didn't answer at first, overwhelmed by the splitting headache and the rush of confusing thoughts. Kenny? Ashton? Cheating? His mind raced, trying to make sense of what Jody had just told him.

"You need to relax," she continued, her tone more cautious now. "I didn't mean to upset you, but you deserve to know the truth."

Camden sat up, gripping the edge of the padded table for support. "Wait—are you serious? Kenny... and Ashton?" He shook his head, trying to sort through the haze of his memory. Nothing came to him, just more confusion and disbelief.

"Why didn't anyone tell me this before?" he asked, his voice strained. "Why would Terrence or my dad... why would they keep this from me?"

Jody hesitated, glancing at the door as if considering her next words carefully. "They probably don't know. I'm the one who caught them in the act. I even have a video to prove it. I know what I saw, Camden. You were furious when I showed you the video before the race. You were ready to confront her, but then the accident happened, and everything got put on hold."

Camden's head swirled with fragmented images but nothing concrete. The idea of Kenny—who had been so supportive and nurturing—betraying him with Ashton seemed impossible. Yet Jody sounded so certain, so sure of what she had seen. "Do you still have the video?" he asked, unsure if he wanted to see it.

Jody nodded slowly. "I do. I wasn't sure if I should bring it up again, but... Camden, you need to decide what's best for you. You deserve the truth, whether you remember it or not."

Camden's heart pounded in his chest, the pain in his head still throbbing. He didn't know what to think or who to believe. Kenny had been there for him during his recovery, helping him with even the smallest things. How could she do that while still hiding something like this?

"I—I need some time to process this," Camden said, his voice shaky.

"Of course," Jody said, stepping back to give him space.

"I'm sorry to hit you with it like this. Just take it easy, okay?"

Camden nodded, but his mind was in turmoil. The more he tried to think, the more the pain pulsed, making it impossible to focus on anything but the possibility that his whole world had been built on a lie.

"Did you drive here?" Jody's voice seemed as if it were coming from a tunnel.

He nodded. "To my dad's office. I walked over."

"Tell you what," Jody said, her voice still sounding warped. "I'll accompany you back when this wave of dizziness has passed. I'll even make home visits from now on, no extra charge."

Chapter Eighteen

Kenny had a doozy of a day. It had been so intense that she hadn't seen three missed calls from Camden, and when she called him back, he didn't answer. She was quite concerned. Letting herself into the house, she realized that he had company. There was talking and laughing and the sound of the television in the background.

She dearly hoped it was not one of Camden's friends who needed her to participate in the conversation. Not today. She was going to shower and hit the bed.

Weary, she walked upstairs, fixing a bright smile, only to stop in her tracks when she saw that Camden's visitor was Jody Levy. Her smile slipped several notches.

"Jody!" Kenny said, hoping her greeting was not as lackluster as she felt. "I see you finagled your way into our home."

"Kenny!" Jody said joyfully, casually lounging in a chair across from Camden.

Camden was looking a little worse for wear.

"You okay, Cam?" Kenny asked, concerned.

Camden looked at her with a difficult-to-read expression—something between confusion and unease. His eyes lingered on her as if he were trying to see something hidden beneath the surface. "Yeah," he muttered, "I'm fine."

But Kenny could tell that wasn't true. Something felt off, and the energy in the room was strange. She shot a glance at Jody, who seemed too comfortable; her casual posture and smug smile were unsettling. It wasn't often that Kenny felt territorial, but seeing Jody in her home next to Camden stirred something deep in her.

"Long day?" Jody asked, flashing that all-too-bright smile as if she hadn't just interrupted the sanctity of their home.

"Yeah, long day," Kenny replied tersely, walking over to Camden and placing a hand on his shoulder. His muscles were tense beneath her touch, and he didn't relax like he usually did. "I didn't know you were expecting company," she added, her eyes flicking to Jody again.

"I wasn't," Camden said, his voice flat. "Jody followed me home after I had a horrendous headache in her office."

"Oh?" Kenny said, eyeing Jody's smug expression. She had finally wiggled her way into their home with the perfect excuse. "Well, I'm glad you're getting the help you need. But you look tired, Cam. Maybe we should call it a night?"

Jody stood up, stretching as if she'd been there for hours. "I was just leaving," she said, her smile never faltering. "Camden's making great progress, by the way. You're taking good care of him." The compliment felt hollow, almost patronizing.

Kenny nodded stiffly. "That's what I'm here for."

Jody glanced between them and grabbed her bag from the floor. "Well, I'll let you two get some rest. Camden, I'll see you the day after tomorrow for your next session. I meant it when I said I would make house calls."

"Right," Camden said, barely looking at Jody as she made her way toward the door.

As soon as the door clicked shut behind her, Kenny turned back to Camden. "She is making house calls now? You seem... off."

Camden didn't answer right away. He stood up, pacing the room slowly. "Jody told me something today. Something that's been messing with my head."

Kenny's heart rate quickened. "What did she say?"

He finally stopped, facing her with a weary, conflicted look. "She said... that you and Ashton were having an affair. That she caught you on video and showed it to me before the accident."

"She really is diabolical," Kenny sighed.

"Is it true?" Camden asked, his voice cracking under the weight of the question. "Did you cheat on me with Ashton?"

"No! Absolutely not," Kenny said, stepping closer to him. "That's insane. Ashton and I—there's nothing going on. I would never do that to you. I love you!"

Camden stared at her, his face clouded with uncertainty. "But Jody said she had proof... a video."

Kenny's heart pounded in her chest. "There is a video of him kissing me. I have an explanation; you won't get it without your memory. Jody has been gunning for us to break up. You are vulnerable right now, and she's taking advantage of that. You have to trust me."

"I don't know if I can. I don't know what to believe anymore."

Tears welled up in Kenny's eyes. "You have to believe me. Don't let her come between us. You and me, we're ride or die, remember?"

"That's the thing," Camden said. "I don't remember. I know that I love you. It's there, even now, thrumming in the back of my brain. I remember bits and pieces about us over the last five years. I remember the day you moved in, your raggedy teddy bear. Strangely enough, where you are concerned, the memories trickle in slowly and steadily. And from what I can remember, I love you without a doubt.

"But Jody's claim—it's throwing me off. I don't have the full picture, and it's driving me crazy. I'm stuck between what I feel and what I don't know."

Kenny sunk down on the sofa and massaged her neck. "Would it make a difference if I said I would never hurt you like that? Ever? I am exhausted and can't plead my case right now. You know what? Maybe I should move out."

"Wait a minute," Camden said. "You can't just jump from 'I am not having an affair' to moving out. I don't want you to move out. At least not yet. What kind of ride or die are you if you just pick up stakes and run at the first argument?"

"This is not our first argument," Kenny chuckled dryly. "But there is something else you don't know about us. Three months ago, I gave you an ultimatum: marriage, or we go our separate ways. Moving out might be preempting your decision about us."

Camden blinked in surprise. "An ultimatum? Marriage or...?"

"Or we go our separate ways," Kenny finished, her voice steady despite the tension in the air. She leaned back, crossing her arms as she looked at him, her exhaustion clear. "I didn't mean it as a threat, but we've been together for years, and I needed to know where you stood. We talked about it, Camden. You said you just needed more time. Then the accident happened, and I haven't brought it up because obviously there would be no point."

Camden stared at her, the weight of her words sinking in. He tried to piece together the fragments of their relationship, but the memories were like slippery glass—always just out of reach. "So I was supposed to make a decision before the accident?" he asked, his voice quieter now.

Kenny nodded. "No, three weeks after the accident, but you lost your memory, and now, with everything happening... with Jody and these doubts, I feel like I'm at a breaking point."

Camden rubbed his hands over his face, groaning in frustration. "This is... a lot. I don't know how I'm supposed to make a decision about something this important when I don't remember anything."

"I know," Kenny sighed, "but maybe this is a sign."

"A sign of what? Don't you love me anymore?" Camden asked.

"I do," Kenny said. "I may love you forever. I just don't think love is enough. I deserve to be proposed to without having to harass you into it. I will forever think I'm the woman who was not good enough to get a spontaneous proposal from the man she loves," Kenny finished, her voice breaking slightly. She tried to hold back the flood of emotion, but the exhaustion from holding it all in for so long was too much. "I don't want to feel like I'm forcing you into something you're not ready for, Camden. I deserve more than that."

Camden looked at her, his heart sinking. He hated seeing her like this, knowing that his uncertainty was causing her so much pain. The truth was, even without his full memory, he could sense that she was right. She did deserve more. But he also couldn't ignore the fog of confusion clouding his mind.

"Kenny, you're more than good enough. You're the best thing that's ever happened to me," he said, his voice low but earnest. "If I haven't proposed yet, it's not because you don't deserve it—it's because I'm a mess. Especially now. I'm trying to piece my life back together, but it feels like everything is slipping through my fingers."

She wiped her eyes, the raw emotion still visible on her face. "I know you're going through a lot. I've been patient, haven't I? But I'm running out of steam, Cam. I can't keep pretending everything's fine when I'm constantly wondering if I'm just waiting for your memory to return, only to find that marriage is one step too far."

Her words cut deep, and Camden felt a pang of guilt. Why hadn't he proposed to Kenny? He loved her—he knew that—but everything else was still blurry.

"I don't want to lose you," he whispered, his voice barely audible. "I don't know what the future holds, Kenny. But I do know that you mean everything to me. I just... I just need more time to figure things out."

Kenny nodded slowly, the resignation clear in her expression. "I understand, Camden. Time is always an issue with us, it seems. Tell you what, I will stay here until you get back your memory, and then I am going to leave. It wouldn't be right for me to leave you while you need me most. I would have stayed with you and helped you through this even if we were not in a relationship. It has always been that way with us, after all."

She got up. "I'll sleep in one of the guest rooms till then."

Camden swallowed. "Kenny…"

She didn't dare look at him before she changed her mind. She had her resolve, and she was sticking to it.

Chapter Nineteen

They had reached an impasse. Their once-perfect relationship had descended into a cold war. Jody was visiting the house every other day, ostensibly to help with Camden's physiotherapy, but she conveniently made him her last client and lingered afterward. She's probably stuffing Camden's mind with lies, Kenny thought snarkily. The tension built in the house every time she saw Jody's car parked outside. It gnawed at her—the uncertainty, the quiet animosity brewing beneath the surface of their interactions. Camden was polite but distant, lost in his own thoughts, while Kenny was painfully aware of how far they had drifted.

On the other hand, Jody found every excuse to stay after Camden's sessions. It was subtle at first—just an extra few minutes here, a cup of tea there—but she had become a regular fixture in their home. The sight of Jody lounging on their couch, laughing with Camden, made Kenny's stomach churn with frustration.

Kenny couldn't shake the feeling that Jody was up to something, playing on Camden's vulnerability to wedge herself into his life.

Physiotherapy was just an excuse to get her foot in the door, she thought bitterly. Jody had always had a thing for Camden, and now that he was vulnerable, she was making her move.

One evening, after a particularly long session with Jody, Camden found Kenny sitting at the kitchen table, stirring a cup of tea absently. She looked up as he walked in, her eyes sharp but her face carefully neutral.

"Hey," he said cautiously.

"Hey," she replied, her voice clipped. "Is Jody gone?"

"Yeah, just a few minutes ago. She was helping with my shoulder again," Camden said, rolling his shoulder as if to prove a point. "It's getting better."

Kenny took a deep breath, forcing herself to keep her tone calm. "Is she going to keep hanging around after your sessions every day? Because it feels like we have a new houseguest."

Camden frowned. "She's just been keeping me company. You're usually busy with work or out. It's nice to have someone to talk to. What's the problem?"

Kenny put her cup down, the tension simmering just beneath the surface. "The problem, Camden, is that Jody isn't just a friend. She's the one who told you I was cheating. And now she's here, in our home, constantly whispering God knows what in your ear. It's not exactly easy for me to deal with."

Camden rubbed the back of his neck, looking conflicted. "I know you don't like her being here, but I'm not going to cut her off just because of something she said."

"Something she said that was a lie," Kenny corrected, her

voice rising slightly. "She's trying to sabotage us, and you're letting her."

He sighed. "I'm not letting her do anything, Kenny. I'm just trying to figure things out, and right now, Jody's the only one who seems to understand what I'm going through."

Kenny stood up, unable to keep her frustration in check any longer. "Of course she does! She's manipulating you, Camden. She's taking advantage of the fact that you're confused, and you're letting her walk right into our lives like it's no big deal."

Camden's expression hardened. "That's not fair. She's helping me, Kenny. You don't get to decide who's here for me and who isn't."

The words hung between them, thick with tension. Kenny crossed her arms, her heart racing. "I'm not going to sit here and watch her destroy what we have, Camden. You need to figure out who you trust, and soon, because I'm not fighting for us against her every day."

Camden didn't respond, his silence saying more than words could.

Kenny turned and left the room, the cool war between them deepening with every step.

****

Camden had developed a new fascination with reading detective novels. They kept his mind from dwelling on the fact that Kenny was mad at him, his father was breathing down his back for him to remember, and he had turned into a recluse, afraid to meet people he knew but didn't remember. Amnesia was a fascinating condition to explore until you had it. Nobody could prepare you for the emotional rollercoaster that came with it. Each page he turned in the novels took him into the minds of characters who were piecing together their own fragmented lives, and for a moment, it felt like he was doing the same. The thrill of the mysteries captivated him, providing a temporary escape from the chaos swirling in his own mind.

But reality had a way of crashing in at the most inconvenient times. As he flipped through the latest novel, a sense of unease settled over him. The fictional detective's struggles seemed trivial compared to his own: the faces he couldn't place, the memories that eluded him like shadows in the night.

He leaned back in his chair, sighing. He wished he could find his own clues and resolution instead of waiting for pieces of his life to miraculously return. The frustration gnawed at him. Every day felt like a fresh reminder of what he had lost—not just memories, but the connection he shared with Kenny, the easy laughter, the intimacy that felt like a second skin.

The detective in his book was uncovering secrets and solving puzzles, but Camden felt trapped in his own unsolvable mystery. What if he never remembered? What if Jody's influence kept pushing him further away from Kenny, leaving him in a state of perpetual uncertainty?

He closed the book and rubbed his temples, trying to fend off the headache that was forming. He needed to talk to Kenny to clear the air. But the thought of facing her and admitting how lost he felt was daunting. Would she even want to hear it?

As he stared out the window at the pouring rain, Camden felt the weight of isolation pressing down on him. He was caught between the man he used to be and the stranger he had become. Perhaps it was time to step out of the shadows to confront the reality of his relationship with Kenny.

Why hadn't he proposed to Kenny before? What was blocking him? His reluctance to commit in a deeper way was obviously hurting her. As for the accusation of her cheating on him with Ashton, he actually believed that she hadn't done it. The Kenny he knew wouldn't have done such a thing, and he was sure she hadn't changed that much.

His phone rang, dragging him from his self-reflection. He took a deep breath and reached for it. It was his dad.

"What are you doing right now, Camden?" his father asked.

"Reading a detective novel, contemplating life," Camden said. "Why?"

"Your vacation is on the brink of being over," Jim said. "I'm sending Ashton over with some papers. I want you to read them and give me some insights. Even if you don't remember the case, I need your brand of outside-the-box thinking right about now."

"Wait! Dad," Camden said. "Do you have any idea why I haven't married Kenny yet?"

"You've told me more than once that you would never get married because of your mother's and my lifestyle."

"Oh, that," Camden said, "your swinger lifestyle."

"Yep," Jim replied. "I dearly and fervently wish you hadn't seen what you did. I also wish your amnesia would have covered that one memory."

"But it didn't," Camden sighed. "And I know. But why would seeing the two of you having sex with other people affect me like this? I am no longer a child; my perceptions have changed."

"Your views on commitment were irreparably shattered," Jim said regretfully. "I don't know what to tell you, son. Maybe you should see a psychotherapist again."

When he hung up, Camden picked up his book and then put it down again. He couldn't get lost in the story anymore.

Instead, he called Rory. To his credit, Rory stayed on the phone with him, keeping him company until the low feeling he had disappeared.

Chapter Twenty

Somebody was pressing the door buzzer unnecessarily long. Camden dragged open the door and glared at the perpetrator.

"I have a delivery for Camden Byfield," Ashton said, raising a box of papers.

"Come on in," Camden grumbled.

He hadn't even sat down properly before the doorbell rang again. He glanced at his phone and saw that it was Jody. They didn't have therapy, and she was dressed up. He wondered, irritatedly, what she wanted.

He opened the door grumpily. Jody greeted him with a bright smile on her face, dressed in a little black dress that hugged her curves closely. "I was thinking that we should go out this evening. I can wait while you get ready."

Camden frowned. "I can't go out. I have work."

"I thought you said you didn't remember work," Jody said as he headed back to the living room.

"Oh wow," Ashton exclaimed when he saw Jody striding

into the living room like a model on a catwalk. "You old dog, you," Ashton said to Camden. "I'm going to tell Kenny that you have strippers coming over for entertainment."

"I am no stripper," Jody growled. "I am his physiotherapist!"

"Oh my, I had no idea," Ashton said exaggeratedly. "So sorry, ma'am. I suddenly feel a pain in my shin. Since you make house calls, can I give you an address?"

"Wait a minute," Jody glared at Ashton. "Aren't you the guy who is having an affair with Kenny behind Camden's back?"

"I wish," Ashton laughed. "I love me some, Kenny, but unfortunately, she loves this guy here."

"I have a video!" Jody said, grabbing her phone. "Of you kissing Kenny after a party and a video of you and her talking and laughing at Mingles."

"Are you sure you don't work for a gossip magazine?" Ashton wiggled his eyebrows. "Why are you so fascinated with taking videos of Kenny? I know she's pretty, but to have a personal stalker?"

"Let me see the video," Camden said, holding out his hand.

Jody showed him the video. Ashton was kissing Kenny passionately, exaggeratedly. She wasn't responding; she looked shocked and frozen in place. Camden studied the video objectively. Wasn't that Audra behind them? This was the video that had caused him to question Kenny's loyalty. He definitely hadn't been thinking clearly when he saw it before.

"Present your case, Jody," Camden said, handing back the phone. "Tell me why you think Kenny was having an affair with my cousin."

"My case?" Jody stammered.

"Yup," Ashton leaned forward. "You accuse me of having an affair with this man's girl. You should have evidence a mile high."

"Well, the video—" Jody started.

"The video proves that I was kissing Kenny," Ashton said. "You've jumped to the conclusion that it was an affair when, in reality, it could be something entirely different. I remember the night vividly. I was trying to escape the clinging talons of one Tori Dasilva, aka Jessica Rabbit, a well-endowed dancer from Sensuous City who had concluded that I was her next relationship, whether I liked it or not.

"Kenny pretended to be my girlfriend and kept her at bay, but alas, the lady was going to follow me home. I saw her and grabbed Kenny, putting on a spectacle that had her convinced enough to leave the place in a huff.

"I will forever be grateful to Kenny for allowing me to kiss her. She said she was going to tell you, Camden, and of course, I had expected to be decked that Monday in the office, but alas, your accident happened, and here we are.

"Well, what about Mingles? I saw you and Kenny talking and laughing when her friend left. You both looked chummy."

"I usually try to be engaging and entertaining whenever I'm spending time with someone I like," Ashton said. "I happen to like Kenny; she is my cousin's girl. By the way, are you single?"

"Me?" Jody stuttered.

"Yep," Ashton said. "I'm not picky. Now and again, I date a crazy chick. I have never dated a crazy physiotherapist before. Does this mean if you drive over my foot, you'll rehabilitate me?"

Camden laughed.

"I am not crazy," Jody said, looking at Camden reprovingly.

Camden wiped a tear of laughter from his eye. "Sorry, it's just that Ashton has a way of making everything sound absurd, even in tense moments."

Ashton flashed a grin. "Glad to be of service. But seriously, Jody, I'm not trying to put you on the spot. I just think you're overstepping your boundaries with Camden and Kenny. This drama isn't helping anyone. Camden is off the market, but I am very much on. You should be considering my eligibility as a potential partner, not him."

Jody crossed her arms and glared at Ashton. "I was just trying to look out for Camden's best interests, not poaching him from Kenny."

Camden leaned forward. "I appreciate the concern, but I trust Kenny. She's been there for me; I love her. Even without my memory, I know that there's no leaving her. I'm sticking to that woman like glue."

Jody sat down abruptly on the sofa. "I guess I'll back off. I'm sorry if I overstepped. I just hated seeing you hurt. I've always had a soft spot for you."

"Good girl," Ashton smiled.

"And on that note, let's leave him to read," Ashton said, leading Jody to the front door. "You're all dressed up; let's go to dinner somewhere. I'm sure after I tell you about how horrible Camden can be, your crush on him will crash. I'm no doctor, but I can mend your broken pieces."

"That's the best you can do in terms of sweet talk?" Jody looked at Ashton skeptically.

"No, I have cornier lines than these," Ashton murmured. "Trust me on that."

****

Camden had fallen asleep on the couch surrounded by papers. He hadn't even heard when Kenny came in.

He cracked his eye open and yawned. "What time is it?" He asked.

Kenny came into his line of sight with a drink in hand and sat across from him. She was in boy shorts and a tiny tank top that barely covered her breasts.

"Wow," he breathed. He almost fell off the settee.

"It's eight o'clock," Kenny said. "I came in, showered, and now I am having a cocktail. I see you were busy today."

"Yes," Camden sat up. "My dad sent over papers for me to peruse." He picked them up and neatly arranged them. "Ashton brought them over."

Kenny nodded. "Okay."

"And Jody was right behind him in a little black dress that showed a lot of skin," Camden said. "It left me cold, but your outfit is heating me up. Come here."

"No," Kenny shook her head. "Tell me what happened when Ashton and Jody showed up first."

"Jody accused him of being your lover behind my back," Camden explained. "Ashton laughed at her nonsense and explained what was happening in the video—he was trying to make some girl jealous by kissing you."

Kenny nodded. "So Jody is finally letting it go?"

"I'd think so. Ashton convinced her to go to dinner with him. He said he likes his women with a hint of crazy."

Kenny chuckled. "And what about you? Are you jealous now that your adoring physiotherapist is otherwise occupied?"

"I only have eyes for you," Camden said.

Kenny smirked, raising an eyebrow. "Really? Just me?"

"Yes," Camden nodded. "It's a conclusion I've came to a long time ago. I asked my dad today why I was reluctant to commit to you."

"And?" Kenny asked.

"And he reminded me about something that happened years ago when I was ten." Camden said, "I walked in on them having an orgy."

Kenny gasped. "What? Your parents? Your happily in love parents?"

Camden nodded. "They do what makes them happy, I guess. As a kid, I was traumatized—it threw me off."

"Oh wow," Kenny whistled. "That must have been intense. I can see why that would mess with your view of relationships."

"Yeah," Camden continued, his gaze dropping to the floor. "It made me question what love really means. I thought maybe love was supposed to be exclusive, just for two people. But seeing them like that... it was a wake-up call. They were happy, and it made me wonder if I was limiting myself. They even sent me to therapy; I think I was a bit traumatized."

Kenny moved over to Camden's seat, placing a reassuring hand on his shoulder. "So, you're saying that seeing them explore their desires made you afraid to commit? Like, if love can look like that, then what's the point of being all in with one person?"

"Exactly," Camden sighed. "I was torn between what I was taught and what I had seen. I don't want to end up like them—always looking for something more, not satisfied with what I have locked into a marriage with someone who couldn't be my everything. I don't want a relationship where I have to be looking outward to be fulfilled. I had to make sure that you were my everything. The thing is, subconsciously, I knew you were my ride-or-die. I knew it five years ago; I know it now, even without my memories."

"Oh, Camden," Kenny pressed her lips to his throat.

"Will you marry me?" Camden whispered.

"Yes," Kenny said, "but I want you to ask again when you have your memories back."

Camden pulled back slightly, searching Kenny's eyes for reassurance. "You really mean that? You're okay with waiting? You gave me an ultimatum, remember?"

Kenny nodded, her gaze steady. "Absolutely. I want this to be real for you, not just a reaction to what you're feeling now. I want you to remember everything we've built together."

A sense of warmth spread through Camden, mingling with the uncertainty that still lingered in his heart. "I'm scared, Kenny. What if my memories don't come back the way I hope?"

"Then we'll create new ones together," she replied, a soft smile breaking through. "We can build a future that's just ours, one step at a time."

Camden took down the straps of her top. "So, what do we do now?"

"Now," Kenny said, leaning in closer, her lips touching his, "we embrace the present. Make love like it's the first time."

Camden smiled, wrapping his arms around her. "I think I can handle that."

"Good," she whispered, "because I'm all in, Camden. Always."

****

Camden regained his memory in the wee hours of the morning, just ten minutes after three. In his dream, he was running down a pathway when he tripped and fell, tumbling into a dark void. Suddenly, flashes of memories flooded his mind—laughter shared with Kenny, late-night talks, their first kiss under the stars. Each image was vivid as if he were reliving those moments.

Gasping, Camden shot upright in bed, his heart racing.

He could remember everything—the good, the bad, the complicated.

Kenny stirred beside him, her brows furrowing as she sensed his distress. "Camden? What's wrong?"

He looked at her, the weight of memories crashing down like waves. "I remember," he whispered, his voice barely above a breath. "All of it."

Kenny's eyes widened, and she sat up, wrapping the blanket around her shoulders. "You do? What do you remember?"

"Everything," he said, feeling a rush of emotions. "The laughter, the arguments, the last five years." He paused, looking deep into her eyes. "I remember asking you to marry me."

Kenny's expression shifted from surprise to something more profound—relief, love, and hope intertwined. "And...?"

"And I meant it," Camden replied, his voice steady now. "I want to marry you, Kenny. I want all of it—every moment, every memory, even the ones that scared me."

Tears shimmered in her eyes as she smiled, and Camden reached out to cup her face. "Will you marry me?" he asked again, his heart pounding with sincerity.

"Yes," she breathed, a radiant smile breaking across her face. "A thousand times, yes!"

At that moment, Camden knew he was ready to embrace not just the past but also a future filled with love, adventure, and the promise of forever.

The End

Dear Reader,

THANK YOU so much for reading Ride or Die, the first book in the Ridgeview series. I truly appreciate the time you've taken to read my work.

Keep reading for an excerpt from the next book in the series, Play For Keeps, Audra and Jairo's story. I can't wait for you to delve into their story as they experience their highs and lows as they navigate love and life in Ridgeview.

Happy reading, and I look forward to hearing your thoughts!

Warmest regards,

Brenda

It was raining heavily. Echoes of thunder rumbled in the background as lightning lit up the night sky. Audra jumped out of bed.

"I have to go home."

"Why?" her bed partner asked sleepily. "You might as well stay the night. It's late."

"No, I can't." Audra groaned. "I have responsibilities."

"What responsibilities?" He cracked an eye open.

"Uhm, work." Audra ran her fingers through her disheveled hair.

"You can't be serious," he murmured. "You work with your parents. You basically have a nine-to-five job."

"That is so not true! Sometimes I help out at the hospital. Unfortunately, there are always sick children who need my help," Audra said. "Where are my clothes?"

"All over the house," he murmured. "I started tearing them off you the moment I answered the door."

Audra groaned. "I'm going to do something about this."

"What?" he chuckled softly, sitting up in bed.

"See a psychiatrist," Audra said. "My mental health is unraveling. I can't keep doing this."

"We're not hurting anybody," he said. "You're still single, aren't you?"

"Yes," Audra hissed. She spotted her underwear near the door. She picked it up and looked at it; it was torn. She might as well bin it. Her blouse was similarly tattered, and her skirt on the stairwell looked a little worse for wear.

"I'm going to have to borrow one of your shirts," she said, turning around and heading for the closet. "My clothes are fit for the waste bin. Such a pity—I loved that blouse."

"I'll buy you a whole wardrobe," he said lazily. "I've been

thinking, we should formalize our situationship."

Audra shrugged into one of his shirts and turned around. The shirt could be a baggy dress; it would have to do. When she went home, she would sneak into the guest house, have a shower, and then collect Jason from her parents' house. It was a weeknight, after all. She only left Jason with them on weekends. They would wonder why she was getting home so late, and she didn't want to lie. What would she say? Mom, Dad, Jairo called, and as usual, I went running. Did someone have a prescription for what she had? She would happily take it. Her resistance to him was somewhere below zero.

"Audra, you didn't respond," he said huskily.

"I'm sorry," Audra said. "I was wondering how I was going to sneak in without my parents' knowing."

"Why are you sneaking around?" He looked at her with narrowed eyes. "You're an adult woman, not a child. What are you hiding?"

"Nothing," Audra said. "I wonder if my shoes are still intact?"

He chuckled. "Audra, can we have a serious conversation?"

Audra inhaled. "Are you going to put on clothes?"

"Okay," he said, getting up.

She averted her eyes. She found him irresistible naked. Then again, she found him irresistible with clothes on, too.

"Okay, all good," he said. "You can look now."

He had pulled on black track bottoms with a matching shirt.

"Can we go downstairs?" Audra asked. "Closer to my car?"

"Sure." He held the door while she passed him.

"Don't touch me," Audra said, her voice brittle.

"I won't," he sighed. "Believe it or not, I've come to the same conclusion you have; we're combustible together. I've never felt like this before. Makes me feel a little out of control."

Audra paused and looked at him. "That's good to know—that this malady isn't only infecting me."

Jairo chuckled. They headed downstairs and into the living room. Audra found her shoes and put them on.

He watched her silently, then said, "I bought a house."

Audra spun around. "Good. Congrats. That's how many houses now?"

"Thirteen," he answered solemnly. "The others are investments. This house I'm talking about is a personal residence—in Jamaica."

Audra looked at him incredulously. "Oh really?"

"Yes," Jairo nodded. "I was thinking I need to move back home, get settled, start a family."

Audra cleared her throat. "Well, that's nice."

"I guess we'll be seeing a lot more of each other," Jairo said.

"Uh-huh." Audra nodded.

"And it would stand to reason since we can't keep our hands off each other, that we should look into making things official," Jairo said.

"Official as in… married?" Audra asked, widening her eyes.

"I never want to get married again," Jairo shrugged. "It wasn't a fulfilling experience. I was thinking more along the lines of us moving in together. That way, you don't have to sneak off into the night."

"I'm not sneaking," Audra said. "Just stealthily approaching the guest house without them seeing me."

"So, what do you say, Audra?" Jairo asked.

"I can't." Audra inhaled raggedly and headed to the front door. "I have a son. I want him to have an example of a stable, committed relationship. I don't want him growing up confused or feeling like things are temporary."

Jairo frowned, stepping closer. "When did you have a son? Why am I just finding out? How old is he?"

Audra inhaled. "He's eight."

"Eight!" Jairo looked at her in disbelief. "You had him while you were in college?"

"Final year," Audra said.

"Who is his father?" Jairo asked quietly.

Audra bit her lip. This was the moment of truth. If she blurted out you, things would forever change.

She hesitated, her heart racing. She could feel Jairo's eyes on her, waiting, expecting an answer. This was the moment she had avoided for years—the truth that would turn everything upside down.

She took a deep breath and finally met his gaze. "You," she whispered.

Jairo blinked, his expression unreadable. "What?" he asked, his voice low.

"You," Audra repeated, her voice firmer this time. "You're his father, Jairo."

Silence fell between them, thick and heavy. Jairo's face shifted from confusion to shock, then anger. "Why didn't you tell me? All these years—" He ran a hand through his hair, pacing in disbelief. "You kept this from me?"

Audra nodded. "Yes, I kept it from you. He was conceived the night of your bachelor party. You were going to marry another woman. You were on your honeymoon when I found out I was pregnant."

"I still had a right to know!" His voice rose, frustration evident. "Eight years, Audra. I've missed eight years of his life!"

"I know!" she said. "I know, and I hate myself for it. But I thought I was doing the right thing at the time. What newlywed man wants to find out that his yearly booty call was pregnant with his child?"

"You were not a yearly booty call," Jairo said savagely. "My feelings for you have always been complicated. I tried to stay away but couldn't. I came out here yearly for no other reason but to see you. At first, I couldn't believe you'd give me the time of day, but when you did, I was hooked." His voice was rough with emotion. "I was hooked on you, Audra. Every time I saw you, it got harder to walk away. I kept coming back because I couldn't imagine not having you in my life, even if it was just for those few stolen moments. I knew you had your plans to marry a fellow doctor and be a power couple."

He paused, then continued, "I only walked away that last time because I overheard you telling someone on the phone that you value brains over brawn and that a relationship with a dumb footballer wasn't sustainable."

Audra closed her eyes in mortification and swallowed. "I wasn't talking about you."

Jairo's jaw tightened, his eyes flashing with frustration. "Then who were you talking about, Audra? Because it sure sounded like you were talking about me. I am a footballer."

Audra exhaled slowly, her voice soft but steady. "I was talking to Travis Pierce. We met at a frat meeting—he was on a football scholarship at university. He thought his looks meant I'd fall at his feet. I insulted him every time he called me. None of my insults landed, especially that one, because he wasn't dumb—far from it. That conversation had nothing to do with you."

Jairo stared at her, his expression still hard. "You really expect me to believe that?"

"Yes, because it's the truth," Audra replied, her voice firm. "I never saw you as just a football player. You were always more than that to me. But you were getting married, and I didn't want to stand in the way of that. I thought... I thought it was best for both of us to move on."

Jairo took a step closer, his voice lowering. "But I didn't move on. I tried, but no one else came close to what we had. I kept thinking about you, about the time we spent together. And now you're telling me that all this time, I had a son I didn't even know about? Do you have any idea how that feels?"

Audra's heart clenched. She reached out, but he took a step back, his emotions too intense for him to let her in. "I didn't know how to tell you, Jairo. I was scared you'd resent me for it, or worse, that you'd reject him. I didn't want to bring that pain into Jason's life."

"I wouldn't have rejected him," Jairo said through gritted teeth, his hands clenched at his sides. "You should've trusted me with the truth, no matter what you thought I'd do."

"I know," Audra whispered, guilt washing over her. "I was wrong. I see that now. But I can't change the past, Jairo. All I can do is try to make things right from here."

Jairo's expression softened just a little, the anger still there but beginning to ebb. "So what now? What are we supposed to do with this?"

Audra took a deep breath, meeting his gaze with sincerity. "We co-parent, I guess. We figure out a way to raise Jason together, even if it's messy. He deserves to know you, and you deserve to know him."

Jairo ran a hand over his face, his emotions warring within him. "And us? What about us?"

Discover Exclusive Offers and Be the First to Know!

If you haven't already, don't miss out on the opportunity to join my New Release Newsletter! Sign up today and become part of an exclusive community where you'll be among the first to hear about my latest book releases and take advantage of special prices.

Why join my mailing list?

Be the First: Get a head start and be the first to know when I release a new book.

Exclusive Discounts: Unlock special prices available only to subscribers. Enjoy limited time offers and save big on your favorite books.

Quick and Easy: Signing up takes less than 30 seconds.

To join, visit https://www.brenalbar.com/newsletter or scan the QR code below.

Thank you for your support, and happy reading!

Ridgeview Series

The Ridgeview series follows five couples on the Jamaican north coast in the luxurious community of Ridgeview. It explores their everyday struggles with careers, children, and family drama. Each book touches on love, marriage, and trust as the characters face challenges that test their relationships.

Ride or Die (Book 1)
Play For Keeps (Book 2)
Through Thick and Thin (Book 3)
Tried and True (Book 4)
Stay With You (Book 5)

Spice and Stone Series

Join three extraordinary girls—Cinnamon, Cayenne, and Sage—as they navigate the intricate flavors of life, love, and romance in the captivating Spice and Stone series.

Cinnamon (Book 1)
Cayenne (Book 2)
Sage (Book3)

The Crimson Hill Series

Where family drama, romance, and a touch of sci-fi blend seamlessly in the enchanting backdrop of a small town in Jamaica. Prepare to embark on an unforgettable journey as secrets unravel, passions ignite, and destinies intertwine.

No Goodbye (Book 1)
No Misunderstanding (Book 2)
No Ordinary Love (Book 3)
No Fairy Tale (Book 4)
No Letting Go (Book 5)
No Strings Attached (Book 6)
No More Mrs. Nice Girl (Book 7)
No Place Like You (Book 8)
Knight and Day (Book 8.5)
No Expectations (Book 9)
Ice and Fyre (Book 9.5)
No Surrender (Book 10)
No Time for Love (Book 11)
No Promises (Book 12)
Winter's Eve (Book 13)

The Wiley Brothers

Step into the world of the Wiley Brothers, where tragedy weaves an unbreakable bond and love becomes their guiding light. In this captivating series, follow the journey of six remarkable boys as they navigate the tumultuous path of growing up without parents, discovering love, and finding their place in a challenging world.

Between Brothers (Book 0)- How it all began…
For Pete's Sake (Book 1)- Preston's story.
Crossing Jordan (Book 2)-Jordan's story.
Fire and Walter (Book 3)- Walter's story.
The Perfect Guy (Book 4)-Guy's Story.
The Patience of a Saint (Book 5)- Saint's Story.
A Case of Love (Book 6)- Case's Story.

The Pryce Sisters

Follow the remarkable journey of the Pryce triplets as they navigate the complexities of growing up, discovering romance, and embracing the exhilarating challenges of the new adult years.

Baby For A Pryce- Book 1
Right Pryce Wrong Time – Book 2
Yours, For A Pryce- Book 3

The Jacksons

Prepare to be enthralled by the captivating saga of the Jackson family. In this gripping series, secrets unravel, paternity questions loom, and love blooms in the most unexpected corners.

Ace- Book 1
Deuce- Book 2
Trey- Book 3
Quade- Book 4

The Scarlett Series

Their patriarch died and unexpectedly left each of them a fortune. Watch as the Scarlett family navigate their way through the ups and downs of sudden wealth, family secrets, and the complicated dynamics of their relationships.

Scarlett Baby (Book 1)
Scarlett Sinner (Book 2)
Scarlett Secret (Book 3)
Scarlett Love (Book 4)
Scarlett Promise (Book 5)
Scarlett Bride (Book 6)
Scarlett Heart (Book 7)

Magnolia Sisters

They were the rejects. The worst of the lot, they grew up in a girl's home together and formed sisterly bonds. Each book in the series tells the story of a different girl and the unique struggles and triumphs she faces along the way. With themes of friendship, forgiveness, and the power of love, the "Magnolia Sisters" series is a heartwarming and inspiring read that you won't want to put down.

Dear Mystery Guy- Book 1
Bad Girl Blues- Book 2
Her Mistaken Dream- Book 3
Just Like Yesterday – Book 4

New Song Series

A group of friends started out as a church band, see how each of them navigate their personal and professional lives while staying true to their faith and facing challenges along the way. With themes of forgiveness, redemption, and second chances, the New Song Series is a captivating read for anyone who enjoys heartwarming stories of love and faith.

Going Solo- Book 1
Duet on Fire- Book 2
Tangled Chords- Book 3
Broken Harmony- Book 4
A Past Refrain- Book 5
Perfect Melody- Book 6

The Bancrofts

The Bancroft family delves into the inner workings of academia and the high-stakes world of university politics. The family wrestles with the pressures of maintaining their family's legacy, they must confront their own demons and navigate the complex relationships that bind them together. From unexpected love affairs and betrayals to scandals and secrets that threaten to tear them apart, this is a series that will keep you captivated until the very end.

Homely Girl- Book 0
Saving Face- Book 1
Tattered Tiara- Book 2
Private Dancer- Book 3
Goodbye Lonely- Book 4
Practice Run- Book 5
Sense of Rumor- Book 6
A Younger Man- Book 7
Just To See Her- Book 8

Three Rivers Series

Three Rivers Series, a captivating tale of love, redemption, and second chances set in a picturesque community in St. Ann's Bay, Jamaica.

Private Sins- Book 1
Loving Mr. Wright- Book 2
Unholy Matrimony- Book 3
If It Ain't Broke- Book 4

The Resetter Series

The Resetter Series takes a look at a rare kind of person, a person who can travel back in time, but they only have one chance to get things right if they go back! With themes of second chances, changing the past and the power of love, the resetters series is a captivating time travel romance that many readers have described as a page turner.

Never Too Late- Book 1
Never Say Never- Book 2
Now or Never- Book 3
Almost Never- Book 4

On the Rebound Series

Experience the gripping and emotionally charged On the Rebound series, where love, betrayal, and redemption collide in a whirlwind of passion and secrets. Brace yourself for a journey filled with drama, cheating scandals, DNA questions, and ultimately, the power of second chances and finding love again.

On the Rebound- Book 1
On the Rebound Book 2

Standalone Books

Full Circle- After graduating from university, Diana wanted to return to Jamaica to find her siblings. What she didn't foresee was that she would meet Robert Cassidy and that both their pasts would be intertwined, and that disturbing questions would pop up about their parentage just when they were getting close.

After the End- Torn between two lovers. Colleen married her high school sweetheart, Isaiah, hoping that they would live happily ever after, but life intruded, and Isaiah disappeared at sea. She found work with the rich and handsome Enrique Lopez as a housekeeper and realized that she couldn't keep him at arm's length.

Love Triangle: Three Sides to the Story- George, the husband. Marie, the wife, and Karen-the mistress. They all get to tell their side of the story.

New Beginnings- Inner-city girl Geneva was offered an opportunity of a lifetime when she learned that her 'real' father was a wealthy man. Her decision to live up-town meant she had to leave Froggie, her 'ghetto don,' behind. She also found herself battling with her stepmother and battling her emotions for Justin, a suave up-towner.

The Preacher and the Prostitute- Prostitution and the clergy don't mix. Tell that to ex-prostitute Maribel, who finds herself in love with the Pastor at her church. Can an ex-prostitute and a pastor have a future together?

Historical Fiction

You won't want to miss out on these two captivating reads!

"The Pull of Freedom" tells the story of a slave family and their desperate struggle for freedom in Jamaica's colonial era. Follow the journey of these brave individuals as they fight for their right to be free, facing danger, heartbreak, and unimaginable obstacles along the way.

"The Empty Hammock" takes readers on a journey through time, as a modern woman finds herself transported back to the Taino era of Jamaica's history. Experience the wonder and mystery of this ancient culture through her eyes, as she learns about their traditions, beliefs, and way of life. With richly drawn characters and a beautifully realized setting, "The Empty Hammock" is a must-read for anyone who loves historical fiction that transports them to another time and place.

Short Story Collections

Di Taxi Ride and Other Stories- Funny stories about Jamaican life to make you laugh.

www.ingramcontent.com/pod-product-compliance
Lightning Source LLC
Chambersburg PA
CBHW061256120726
48001CB00001B/325